CW00689973

**THIS IS A REVISED \
DELIVERY' WITH NE
NOVELLA WAS FIRS1 1 UBLISHED IN 2015 BY
ENDEAVOUR PRESS.**

Susan Willis   www.susanwillis.co.uk

The characters, premises, and events in this book are fictitious. Names, characters, and plots are a product of the author's imagination. Any similarity to real persons, living or dead, is coincidental and not intended by the author.

Chapter One

Michael Philips looked at his naked wife, Davina sitting on the edge of the bed. She'd woken with the alarm, thrown the quilt aside and swung her legs off the bed. He stared longingly at her long slim back and elegant neck which was still tanned from their holiday in Turkey.

She leant forwards and stretched her arms out sighing softly. There wasn't one occasion in seven years of marriage that he could ever remember not wanting her. In his eyes, she was the crème de la crème.

He ran his middle finger down her spine, and she shivered slightly in response. Was this the green light, he wondered and decided to chance his luck. He leant forward, tickled her under the arm and pulled her backwards onto the bed. 'Come on, Dee,' he laughed. 'We've got half an hour?'

He'd obviously misjudged the situation because she gave him a glassy stare, tutted in annoyance, and pushed him away.

She got up from the bed. 'No, Michael, I need to shower and be at work early this morning.'

She walked to the tallboy and pulled a bra and pair of knickers from the drawer while he raised himself up on his elbow. He looked in the mirror of the dressing table and saw her naked. Everything about her was exquisite and he groaned, 'But it's been two weeks now!'

She turned around to face him and put her head on one side. 'Look,' she said. 'Let's see what tonight brings, eh?'

But he didn't want to wait until tonight. He wanted her now. He gave her what he hoped was a suggestive look as she walked towards him clutching her underwear. Her shoulder length blonde hair was dishevelled, and her blue eyes looked sombre, but she did smile at him with her small rose-bud lips. They were the most glorious thing about her face.

She bent forward and kissed him on the forehead, then whispered. 'Tonight, love, I promise.'

What was that all about? Why was she kissing him like an aunt would do when he was a little boy? He searched her face looking for something. Anything that would explain why she didn't want him. Because this wasn't the first time, she'd knocked him back. It was beginning to be a regular occurrence.

She continued through into the en suite, and he scrambled off the bed to follow her, but she closed the door quietly just before he got there.

***

His mood blackened with frustration as he stared at the white wood door. He ground his teeth and turned abruptly stomping along the hall into the bathroom to shower. Standing under the hot water he let it stream down his face and then lathered his short hair with shampoo. And, another thing, he moaned, why was she suddenly closing doors? They'd always been free and easy with each other's bodies. He frowned knowing there was something seriously wrong between them.

She hadn't been interested in making love for weeks now and even on holiday when they had, she'd seemed distant. He remembered how they'd left the beach covered in sand and hurried back to the hotel room then he'd pulled her into the shower with him. They'd washed each other and he had gathered her up in his arms then worried her to the bed.

When he'd kissed her and roamed his hands over her body, she had responded greedily but he had known her mind was elsewhere.

He towelled himself dry now and headed back into the bedroom for clean clothes. It would be best to leave it until later when he could talk to her properly, he decided. He had to find out what was going wrong between them.

***

They were having a true Indian summer and even though it was the last few days of September the sun was breaking through the clouds when he climbed into his red BMW. He found his sunglasses in the glove compartment, put them on and looked at his face in the rear-view mirror.

He'd planned to trim his goatee beard this morning but because of the distraction with Davina he had forgotten. He would have to remember tonight, he thought, turning on the ignition because she hated it when it was too long and scratchy. He pulled out of the cul-de-sac and drove out of Birstall village towards the factory where he worked as a process technologist.

Parking outside the reception doors he got out of the car and inhaled the familiar smell of fresh meat which wafted in the air from the back of the factory. They produced turkey and pork joints for all the major retailers, and it was heading towards their busiest time of year, which was Christmas.

He hurried through the main doors and then breezed into the small office he shared with his colleague, Anthony.

'Morning,' he called as cheerfully as he could manage.

Anthony glanced up from his computer and smiled. 'Morning,' he said. 'You look rough?'

Michael grimaced. 'I know, more aggravation at home.'

Anthony was fifty-six, bald, and Davina had once said he had a face like a little Irish elf. He had worked for the company for over twenty years and Michael couldn't list the knowledge he'd learned from him.

Anthony resumed typing quickly but nodded his head in understanding.

Michael sat down at the only other desk in the corner with his back to Anthony and booted up his computer. They often sat like this for hours in harmony planning factory trials and processing documents. Someone had once suggested moving their desks so they would be facing one another but they'd shaken their heads in unison. They were happy the way they were.

Michael said, 'She just looks so miserable all of the time. She has no interest in the house, or me for that matter.'

Anthony sighed. 'Well, it's understandable that she's not fired up about the house. I mean, it's taken you two years to get everything the way you want it,' he said. 'There can't be any rooms left to decorate, are there?'

Michael scan-read emails then turned slightly in his chair to face him. 'I know, but surely now the town house is perfect she should be enjoying it?'

Anthony sat forward with his short legs splayed open and rested his elbows on his knees. He made a steeple with his fingers. 'Well, what do you expect her to do? Go from room to room cooing with delight,' he said. 'She's probably just settling in, and if she's being quiet, it could be a sign of contentment.'

Michael thought about this theory but decided he could tell the difference between contentment and uninterested boredom. 'Hmm, maybe I'm making mountains out of molehills,' he said. 'But there's one room she certainly doesn't want to be in and that's the bedroom!'

Anthony lowered his head and looked down. 'Aahh…' he muttered.

Michael felt guilty. He shouldn't be bothering Anthony about his sex life but felt if he didn't talk to someone his head would explode. 'Sorry, mate. It's just that this is the start of our best week, if you know what I mean,' he said then shuffled uncomfortably on the rigid plastic chair. 'Usually, she has the calendar in the kitchen marked with big crosses and checks her temperature regularly. But since late June the calendar is blank, and I've never seen her use the thermometer once.'

Anthony scratched his thick grey beard and looked up at Michael's wall planner with the large black crosses he'd made with a marker pen. 'So, maybe she just wants a break from trying for a baby? The pressure on her must be enormous.'

Michael felt the hairs bristle on the back of his neck and raised his eyebrows. 'She's not the only one under stress here,' he said and ran a hand over his sweaty forehead. 'I'm the one who has to perform every time and I'm not complaining.'

Anthony held up his hands in surrender. 'Hey, I was only saying…'

Michael's cheeks flushed. He was snapping at his good friend unnecessarily who was only trying to help. He could feel the knot of tension in the side of his neck begin to throb. He'd had it since they arrived home from holiday and had been blaming the two suitcases he carried. But now, he decided, it was simply stress and frustration.

He looked down at his factory-issue work boots and mumbled, 'Sorry, I'm just so worried about her!'

'Yeah, of course, you're bound to be, let's get this morning's work organised,' he said. 'It'll help to keep it off your mind for a while.'

Chapter Two

Davina heard Michael's car pull away from the outside of the house and she padded back into the bedroom. She knew hiding from another confrontation with her husband was pathetic and she was being foolish but didn't know how to explain the way she felt.

She thought of his morning attempts to rouse her and wanted to scream. She hated it when he was so needy and tried to touch her which was constant during this week of the month. He was unrelenting. She knew he was desperate for a baby, and so was she, but it just wasn't happening.

She sighed heavily, plopped down onto the stool in front of the dressing table and looked around the room. They'd painted the whole room white. Michael had sneered at first saying it would look bedazzling but once she'd added the soft grey carpet, bedding, and table lamps he'd had to admit it was peaceful and serene.

She began to dress and determined to make it up to him tonight. It wasn't that she didn't love him because she did. However, making love, dare she even think it, had become so routine. When they made love now it was to make a baby it wasn't because she was full of desire and lust. And she didn't think he was either.

Davina stared at her face in the mirror. Surely this happened to most couples in their thirties when they'd been married a while, didn't it? Or was this what everyone called the seven-year itch? She shrugged her shoulders. All she knew was that she felt a large bubble of excitement inside her wanting to break free. She didn't want to plan and always be in the safety of a bed in the dark. She remembered their holiday in Turkey.

They'd been sunbathing all day on a quiet secluded beach. She'd looked at his slim, toned body lying on the sun lounger and had longed to touch him. The desire had built until she wanted him so badly, she couldn't think of anything else. They'd been covered in sand and were hot and sticky. She had wanted to ease his speedo's aside and climb on top of him.

'But I don't want to wait until we get back to the room,' she'd cooed running her hand inside his trunks. He'd been appalled at the thought of doing it on the beach. Even though she had pleaded that no one was in sight, he had insisted upon going back to their room by which time the urge of lust and recklessness had left her.

She sighed heavily. How did she tell him that she longed for change? He would want to know why, after years of happy marriage, now it suddenly wasn't enough. And she wouldn't be able to answer him because she didn't know herself. She couldn't think of a way to tell him without being hurtful. She pushed it from her mind, finished dressing for work in blue trousers and a crisp white shirt then hurried out to her car.

***

When she'd been promoted last year to the managers post on the orthopaedic ward where she had worked for ten years, she had spent the extra money on a new mini. It was cream with a beautiful caramel colour interior, it drove like a dream, and she loved it. Michael had told her to spend the money on what she wanted because she'd worked extremely hard to get where she was now.

She pulled out onto the main road and twinges of guilt niggled in the back of her mind. Any other woman would kill to have Michael as a husband, and she was being unfair to him. She also knew most of her friends thought she was spoilt, which, she decided, she probably was.

The traffic heading into Leicester was heavy, and she sat in a queue at lights turning green to red without moving. She drummed her fingers on the steering wheel and watched a young woman pushing her baby in a buggy along the pavement towards the park.

A lump of misery gathered in the back of her throat, and she moaned softly, why couldn't she do it? She was successful at everything else in her life except the basic female task of getting pregnant. They'd both been checked out by the doctors who had told them there was no reason why they couldn't make babies. She'd followed all the guideline's month after month, but nothing happened.

She was beginning to hate this week now and the sight of the calendar on the wall in the kitchen filled her with dread. The blank boxes with the crosses seemed like a recording of her constant failure. She thought of them as a row of hurdles she had to climb over repeatedly. Then later in the month when she had period cramps she felt as if she'd fallen flat on her face, and everyone was laughing at her pathetic attempts. The cars in front of her moved and she wiped her damp eyes with the back of her hand.

When she drove into a parking space at the back of the hospital surgical block, she saw her new male staff nurse climbing off the back of his red and white, Yamaha motorbike and waved at him. She smiled to herself. Why wasn't she surprised to see him riding something so strong and powerful. It suited his personality perfectly.

He waved back and she realised he was waiting for her to walk into work together. She gathered her bags, climbed out of her mini and saw him swagger towards her carrying his large grey helmet.

Stewart Dunn was charm on legs. He casually flirted with her every time she saw him but so far, she was managing to ignore him. When he'd first started on the ward six weeks ago the flirting had irritated her, but it was done with such a happy, carefree manner that now she found herself enjoying his attention and looking forward to seeing him. It brightened her day.

'Morning,' he said looking her up and down. 'Navy and white, which is a lovely combination. Smart, yet casually on-trend.'

She giggled and shook her head in mock disapproval. 'Stewart, really you shouldn't make comments like that.'

He took the heavy briefcase from her hand to carry. 'Hey, it's a compliment,' he said cheerfully walking ahead. 'Go with them because you never know when they'll come to an end.'

She began to walk alongside him while he swung her briefcase in his large hand as if it was an empty plastic bag. Stewart wasn't a good-looking man, not compared to Michael, but he had a certain large ruggedness which coupled with his gentle caring nature when attending to patients was a heady combination. The rest of her nurses on the ward had nick-named him the gentle giant.

They walked through the main entrance into the early hustle and bustle of the hospital getting ready to open its doors. Porters were pushing tall breakfast trolleys up towards the lifts, patients in dressing gowns were slowly stretching their legs and walking to the hospital shop and Stewart greeted them cheerfully.

He took a deep breath and held his nose in the air sniffing. 'Hmm, what a lovely hospital smell,' he said grinning. 'A mixture of disinfectant and scrambled egg?'

They laughed together and got into the staff lift where she pushed the button for the second floor. She nodded. 'You're right. I've always loved the smell of a hospital ever since I first started on the wards in my training.'

He studied her and she felt the hairs on the back of her neck tingle under his scrutiny. He placed the case on the floor and when he moved his arm, she could smell the

leather from his old biker's jacket. It was black and padded
with studs on the back which had worn away with age.

'Hmm, I can just imagine you in your white uniform,' he
said staring into her eyes.

She looked into his large oval eyes with incredibly long
eyelashes and returned his stare. Their eyes locked. Her
heart was thumping, and the palms of her hands began to
sweat. While the lift moved slowly upwards, she parted her
lips to speak but couldn't. She wanted to reprimand him for
being suggestive and cheeky but felt transfixed by him and
didn't want to be the first to look away.

Suddenly the lift bleeped to tell them they'd reached the
second floor and the doors swung open. He looked startled
then handed her the briefcase and hurried out ahead. 'See
you later,' he called. She heard the uncertainty in his voice
as if he too were shocked at what they'd both just
experienced.

Chapter Three

Michael and Anthony stood in the factory. The noise from the machinery and three production lines was too loud for Michael to hear what Anthony was saying and he pulled him by the arm into the prep room on the side. This small room was filled with trolleys full of ingredients to make stuffing that would be used in the turkey breasts.

'Let's do the stuffing trial first today,' Michael said. 'It's too busy in there now. I'll try and find the new production manager later to ask for a slot when we can run the new recipe.'

Anthony nodded. 'Good idea, have we got everything we need?'

'Yeah, it's all piled up in the hold area,' Michael said. 'I'll bring it through while you get the tumbler ready.'

While Michael deposited the quantities of butter, olive oil, cubed smoked pancetta, onion, garlic, fennel, sage, and fresh breadcrumbs into the front of the tumbler Anthony adjusted the settings on the side. 'Shall we start with a two-minute gentle mix at first?'

Michael agreed and when the mix deposited into a large stainless-steel tub, he inhaled the aromas. 'Yep, it smells good. When I saw how the retailer had asked for the addition of fennel, I wasn't sure, but this could work really well.'

This was the part of the job that Michael loved. The chefs all made 1 Kilo recipes in the kitchen, but it was his responsibility to take the recipes, scale them up to 100 Kilo quantities that would work in the production equipment.

'Hello,' a female voice called from the doorway and they both looked up to see a lady in the obligatory white coat and mop cap. She advanced towards them, and Michael looked down on her petite five-foot-one frame and soft hazel eyes.

'Hi, I'm Stella the temporary production manager. And you two must be our process technologists?'

She held out a small hand to shake and Michael took it in his. Towering above her at six-foot-two he had to bend down slightly to speak to her.

Both men introduced themselves and explained the new recipe they were trialling.

Stella nodded then suggested a more convenient time for them to stuff the turkeys in the production area when it would be quieter.

She smiled at Michael with a definite twinkle in her eye. 'And would it be possible for me to come up to the development kitchen later when you cook the turkey and stuffing. I'd love to taste it?' she said slowly and moistened her full lips.

Michael liked her immediately. She seemed easy to talk with and extremely friendly. 'Yes, of course, we'd like that. It's always good to get second opinions. Me and Anthony are so used to making stuffing's every year we get a little blasé.'

'I can't imagine you being laid back about anything,' she teased looking him up and down. Michael looked into her bright eyes and saw her pupils enlarge and her face flush.

No, he thought, she couldn't be flirting with him, could she? Women didn't usually react like this around him. He quickly glanced over his shoulder to see if another man had entered the room. But all he saw was Anthony grinning at him.

She made to move away. 'Great. I'll look forward to it. Will you ring me on my mobile and let me know what time?'

He nodded dumbly and Anthony bid her farewell as she went back into the production area. Anthony hooted with laughter, and he knew it was because of the astonished look on his face.

Anthony chortled. 'She fancies you!'

Michael tutted. 'Don't be ridiculous,' he puffed but pulled his shoulders back all the same.

They cleared up after the trial and wheeled the tub of stuffing into the chiller to use later in the afternoon. Anthony closed the door behind them and teased, 'A knockback and come on all in the same morning. You're really doing well today!'

'It's not funny!' Michael snorted when they left the production area but then couldn't help laughing along with him.

Chapter Four

Davina was still in a tizzy when she reached her small office at the end of the ward. It wasn't an office as such she kept telling everyone but more of a cupboard with a desk in the middle. In the summer it was stifling hot with no windows and in the winter, it was perishing cold without heating.

She dropped her briefcase onto the desk and booted up her computer wondering what had just happened to her. And indeed, to him, because she was certain he'd felt the same. Park it up, she thought, and get yourself ready for the meeting in ten minutes.

When she returned two hours later, the junior sister on the ward, Lisa, put her head around the door and asked, 'Coffee?'

Davina sighed. 'Oh, I'd love one,' she said plopping down into the chair. It seemed lately that there were so many meetings to go to every day that her job had little to do with patients anymore.

She thought of Stewart imagining her in a white uniform and remembered her early days. She'd loved the job in her training and then qualifying as a junior staff nurse. She had worked hard and long hours excelling in ward management. Her mentor at the time had said her organisational skills were second to none.

Davina had wanted to influence the way her patients were cared for and was quickly promoted. However, there were times when she missed the hands-on part of the job now and was becoming disillusioned in the meetings.

Lisa reappeared with two mugs of coffee and sat down on the only other chair behind the door. Lisa asked. 'Tough one?'

Davina smiled at her friend. Lisa was thirty-six, divorced and was raising her three children alone. She was a good nurse and had been a close ally for the six years they'd worked together.

'Yeah, it's just frustrating more than anything else,' Davina said. 'We are trying to suggest improvements but just get battered with budgets all the time.'

Lisa sighed. 'I don't know how or why you even want to do the blooming job?'

Lisa's pretty face clouded with what would look like bitterness to other people, but Davina knew her better. Her apparent hard exterior was a camouflage for her compassionate soft centre. As the saying goes, she thought, Lisa had a heart as big as a lion.

'I'm beginning to wonder myself, Lisa,' she muttered sipping her coffee.

Lisa tugged at her white tunic stretched tight across her bulging midriff and looked at her with eyes full of concern. 'It's more than that, though, isn't it?'

Davina knew there was no point in trying to hide her other worries because Lisa would see straight though her.

She nodded her head and sighed. 'It's the baby-making thing with Michael again. It's just not happening and the more we try the more frustrated he gets and, the more I'm beginning to dread it,' she said. 'Oh, why can't I do it?'

She choked back the tears which threatened to escape and looked anxiously past Lisa towards the open door. Lisa followed her eyes and kicked the door closed with her flat brown brogue. 'Look, love, it'll happen. Just try to relax.'

She frowned and clenched her jaw. 'Lisa, if one more person tells me to relax, I'll scream!'

Lisa got up from her chair and put her arm along her shoulder. 'I know. I'm sorry that was a rubbish answer, but I don't know what else to suggest.'

Davina sighed heavily and shook her head. 'No, I'm sorry I shouldn't have snapped,' she said. 'Two years ago, when we started trying in earnest it was a new challenge. I was excited waiting for the first few months, but then I'd get upset when the period came and tried not to cry in front of him. But now it's just seems like the norm to be ratty and horrible every month no matter how many times we do it!'

She swallowed down the tears and Lisa squeezed her shoulder in comfort. 'I know, it must be awful for you. And as I've said many times before, it's a crying shame because you'd make a lovely Mum.'

She could feel Lisa's chubby arm which reminded her of her mum, and she grabbed a tissue from the box striving not to break down. She blew her nose hard and took a deep breath.

With a more upbeat tone in her voice, she mocked, 'I mean, it's not like I want a hoard of them like Michael does, that would terrify me, but just one would do!'

Lisa grinned and tilted Davina's face up with her finger. 'Well, you can always borrow one of my little blighters, if you want?'

'Aah, they're not blighters, they're lovely, as well you know it,' she said feeling better and wanting to change the subject.

She asked. 'How are things out on the ward this morning?'

They discussed the morning's theatre list and the consultants ward round which would take place after lunch then Lisa drained her coffee. 'I'd better get going and leave you to it. I've got to arrange to see some upset relatives.'

'Do you need me to come?' Davina asked hoping she would agree. It would be lovely to feel wanted and useful again.

But Lisa shook her head. 'No, thanks, I've got it covered. Stewart's going to help me,' she said.

Davina noticed how her face lit up when she said his name. Had Lisa fallen under the same spell as the junior nurses? And, if that were true, she would be astounded because since the day Lisa's husband had walked out, she'd been bitterly averse to every man within a ten-mile radius.

Chapter Five

Michael lifted the turkey out from the oven in the small development kitchen. He stuck a probe into the thickest part of the turkey breast and when the temperature reached over 78* C he knew it was well cooked.

The aroma of cooked turkey filled the kitchen and wafted down the corridor which brought Anthony hurrying along from the office.

'Mmm, smells great, shall I ring Stella,' he asked with a mischievous look on his face. 'Or do you want to?'

Michael frowned. 'You can,' he grumped. 'I'm not interested.'

Stella walked into the kitchen looking around and smiled. 'Oh my, this is small but perfectly formed, isn't it?'

Anthony agreed and Michael couldn't stop himself smiling at her. In a dark green trouser suit and a loose white blouse, he noted that she was slim with a mass of shiny copper curls and large pink framed glasses.

Michael picked up a sharp knife and carved the turkey expertly while she chattered easily with Anthony.

'Well, I can see you've done this before, Michael?' She simpered.

He could see her looking at his arms and steady hand holding the knife. Michael placed a thick slice of turkey and a good serving of stuffing onto a disposable plate and handed it to her. 'Yeah, it's something I do all year round, so one could say I have plenty of experience '

He had sounded quite stilted but meant it in a polite manner not wanting to encourage her. But when he heard Anthony sniggering behind him, he realised the connotation and fumed. His face flushed and sweat stood along his white shirt collar making him feel uncomfortable.

She took a mouthful, chewed, and then sighed sweetly. 'Mmm, that's a lovely flavour,' she said. 'I can't think I've had fennel before but it's something I'll definitely try again. Have we used it in production before?'

Anthony began to explain that it would be a new ingredient and that the technical team would investigate any significant challenges.

Michael gazed at her animated face. He could tell she had a bubbly personality which was refreshingly new in a team of staff that he'd worked alongside for years.

She nodded. 'So, when will this launch? I hear the factory is incredibly busy in the run up to Christmas, is that right?'

Michael smiled. 'Yeah, we work flat out from the start of November until Christmas Eve,' he said. 'By then, most people have bought their turkeys and done their last big food shop before the big day itself.'

Anthony's mobile rang and he excused himself leaving the kitchen while Michael helped himself to a slice of turkey. He rolled the stuffing around his mouth relishing the combination of flavours. He saw her gazing at his mouth and throat while he swallowed the meat which made him squirm and shuffle his leather shoes on the floor tiles making a squeaky sound.

'Well, if you're always so busy I bet you hate Christmas?' she asked quietly.

Unable to stop himself he grinned at her. 'Oh no. I don't mind being busy, it's my favourite time of year. I love Christmas, always have done and I can't see that changing. We're very traditional at home with old fashioned cards, a real tree and the same baubles are given an airing every year,' he said imaging the scene.

Gazing sentimentally above her head, he said, 'We have the same decorations and lights, watch our favourite TV programs, go to church and have Turkey on Christmas Day of course, and then a joint of pork on Boxing Day.'

She glanced down at his left hand and stared at his wedding ring. 'And does your wife love the same things every year, too?'

For one split second he couldn't grasp what she meant then suddenly remembered Davina mentioning a purple tree last year and how she thought it would fit in perfectly with the décor in the lounge. But she'd only been joking, hadn't she?

'Well, I'd better be off,' Stella said.

She thanked him again for the tasting and left him standing in the kitchen thinking about Davina and their usual Christmas.

Was she happy with the same rituals every year? He was and didn't want to change a single thing but maybe he should ask if she wanted to do things differently. They were both only children and always had both sets of parents to their home for the entire day. He cooked Christmas lunch and proudly showed off the stuffing's he'd been working with and cooked the turkey to perfection. He couldn't think of one thing that he would want to change. It was perfect the way it was, wasn't it?

He shook his head and tutted. It was Stella putting strange imaginings into his head that was making him doubt himself, he thought then cleared away the remains of the turkey. He sighed; he'd have to be careful with this new manager.

Driving home from work he bought Davina her favourite Hotel chocolates and a large bouquet of white roses which she loved. He couldn't think of anything he'd done to annoy her since their holiday, but if they would help get him back into her good books again and put a smile back on her face, they'd be well worth the money.

He was praying she'd want to make love tonight because she was going away for the weekend to Leeds, and this would be their last chance in what they call, the good week. Of which, they hadn't done it once so far.

Michael pulled up outside their three-storey town house. He remembered, at first, how they would be at it every night in the good week. So much so, that his legs were tired at work, and he'd had to ask for a night off.

Humph, he muttered under his breath walking up the drive. How could they have gone from that to this? She was never going to get pregnant at this rate. He put his key into the shiny lock on the black painted front door and entered the downstairs lobby then climbed slowly up the stairs into the open plan lounge.

It was a beautiful room furnished with her good taste in light shades of lilac and darker streaks of purple in the accessories. He placed the bouquet in the kitchen sink with an inch of water, made himself a coffee and sat down to wait for her to come home. At seven o'clock he read her text apologising that she was late and how she would stop off to bring pizza take-out.

Watching rugby on TV he grumbled with the thought of another fast-food night and wished he'd bought something on the way home to cook.

'If you'd let me know earlier that you would be so late, I would have cooked something,' he said poking at the dried-up pizza on his plate. It was like chewing rubber, he thought miserably.

He saw her avoid his eyes and take a deep breath as though she was trying not to argue. 'I've said I'm sorry, Michael. Time just slipped away when I was writing a talk for the seminar next week,' she said. 'It's an awful pizza, shall I make us a sandwich instead?'

He grunted but decided being grumpy wouldn't get her on the right track. He smiled, reached across the table, and stroked the back of her hand. 'No, it's okay. In fact, I've got something for you as a nice desert which will make up for it,' he said and disappeared into the kitchen. This would get her in the mood, he thought excitedly returning with the flowers and chocolates.

'But it's not my birthday until Monday?' She cried burying her nose in the blooms and breathing in deeply. 'Ah, they're beautiful,' she whispered.

He saw her eyes widened in delight at her favourite white chocolates lying on the table. He moved behind her and draped his arm casually along her shoulders. 'Two days early, but hey, what does that matter,' he said and slid his hand down into her shirt. 'We could eat the chocolates upstairs in bed?'

He felt her startle and recoil away from his fingers. It was as if she'd been stung by a wasp.

Her eyes and face were contrite, and he could tell she wanted to make amends. 'Oh, sorry, I…I just wasn't expecting your cold fingers,' she gabbled then lowered her head.

Michael watched her bite the inside of her lip. What was wrong with her, he thought and awkwardly removed his hand then straightened his back. He placed both his hands onto the back of her chair and gripped it tight staring at his white knuckles. He had to get to the bottom of this. 'What's wrong, Davina?'

She shook her head slightly using her long hair as a shield and continued to gaze down at the chocolates on the table. She looked as though she was miles away.

Suddenly, she looked up and as if bringing herself back to the here and now. She swung around in the chair and stared at him. 'It's nothing, Michael. I'm just really tired.'

He took his hands from the chair and placed them on his hips. 'Well, I don't think so, you've been tired before and it's never stopped you. It's as if you don't want to be anywhere near me?' He pleaded, 'Talk to me, Dee, whatever's wrong I know we can fix it.'

Her eyes filled with sympathy, and he recognised the caring look that she used with her patients. She caught hold of his hand, kissed the palm, and placed it on the side of her face. 'I'm sorry, I've upset you and that's the last thing I want to do. Of course, I want you near me,' she said. 'You're my husband, Michael. And I love you.'

He ran his other hand into her soft hair and twirled the strands between his fingers. Maybe, he was overreacting, and she was only tired. He bent forward and kissed the tip of her nose. 'You sure?'

'Of course, I am, you silly goose.'

'Okay,' he muttered nodding slowly.

He watched her take a sigh of relief and felt like one of her patients being reassured and comforted. But he wasn't a patient, and he was not ill. All he wanted was his wife back.

'Now, I have to get moving upstairs to pack my weekend bag for tomorrow,' she said and let go of his hand.

He frowned, pulled back from her and carried the left-over pizza box into the kitchen.

Chapter Six

The following morning, she sat next to him in the car as he drove her into Leicester to the train station.

When he'd gone upstairs last night, she'd been lying asleep on the bottom of the bed curled up into a ball in her underwear. Her trousers and shirt were on a heap on the floor and her pyjamas were next to her on the bed.

She'd obviously fallen asleep getting ready for bed, he'd thought, picked her up and laid her down tucking the quilt around her. She had wrapped her arms around his neck and kissed him goodnight then snuggled herself into his chest with her long legs in between his. This was how they'd slept together when they were first married. He'd murmured, 'I love you,' into her hair deciding she really did look exhausted.

It was now just after seven when they drove past the Grand Union Canal which ran through the bottom of the village. He watched a solitary barge making its way down the canal creating gentle ripples in the water and said, 'Isn't it quiet at this time on a Saturday morning?'

He didn't want her to go and looked at her from the corner of his eye.

'Well,' she said smiling at him while he drove. 'I could have taken a taxi then you wouldn't have lost your weekend lie-in?'

He squeezed the inside of her thigh and ran a finger along the seam of her black jeans. 'It's fine, I'll go for a run when I get back then drop down to Mum for breakfast.'

A light drizzle had begun, and Michael cleared the windscreen with his wipers. 'It looks like you all might get wet if these showers turn heavier, have you got an umbrella?'

She nodded. 'Yeah, but it won't matter because we'll be in the shops most of the day and the hotel is central to the club they've chosen.'

He raised an eyebrow. 'You're going to a night club?'

She giggled and patted his knee. Yes, grandpa, it is a hen party and Lisa has all kinds of fun lined up,' she said. 'Although if I feel as tired as this I'll probably leave after one drink and dance then be back in the hotel asleep by midnight.'

He smilcd. 'Well, ring or text if you want, I'll just be having a few pints with my dad.'

Pulling up outside the train station he wished once more that she wasn't going. She felt closer to him now than she had done for weeks, and he was sure that he could have got them into the bed again. However, because she wouldn't be home until late Sunday, he sighed then lifted her bag out of the boot. Which meant they would be into another week without making love.

'Hiya, sexy!' Lisa called hurrying across the car park towards them. Dressed in pink cut offs and T-shirt she was carrying five, good luck helium balloons. She had the strings clasped firmly in one hand while pulling her trolley holdall with the other. Michael chuckled to himself and shook his head in disbelief. He adored Lisa.

Davina smiled at her while she stood up on tip toe to peck Michael on the cheek and tease him. He took both their bags and carried them onto the platform. At the sound of female laughter, they turned to see more junior nurses arriving along with the hen.

When the train pulled onto the platform, she kissed him farewell, and he lifted their bags into the vestibule wishing them a wonderful time then slowly made his way back along the platform.

Chapter Seven

Davina climbed up the step onto the train and watched the back of Michael walk away. She thought of last night and cringed. When he'd slid his hand down her shirt, she had got a shock but the involuntary reaction to his touch had unnerved her. It had never happened before. Her chest had shivered from where his fingers had been, and she hadn't known what to say to him without being hurtful. She'd had no desire whatsoever to make love. But when she'd looked into his large grey eyes then noticed the frown on his forehead, she had felt terrible for causing him grief.

She walked through into the carriage and consoled herself that at least she'd managed to reassure him.

Davina counted five of the nurses from her ward that had already found seats. She realised they were one short. 'Where's Ellie?' she asked Lisa who was battling to get the balloons through the sliding door into the carriage.

'Oh,' Lisa said puffing with exertion. 'Didn't I tell you she's had to cancel at the last minute? But Stewart is coming instead.'

Davina's stomach did a quick somersault at the sound of his name. 'Stewart!' She exclaimed. 'On a hen party?'

One of the nurses shouted, 'Yeah, he's going to let the bride practise kissing him!'

The hen howled with laughter, 'God, as if I need to practise, we've been shacked up for three months now!'

Davina slumped down next to Lisa who was tying the strings of the balloons to the plastic moulding on her seat.

'I thought I'd told you yesterday, but maybe I forgot?' Lisa said. 'Ellie had paid for the hotel and train, so it seemed silly to waste the money.'

Davina removed her jacket and stowed it in the overhead rack. 'Well, where is he?'

'Oh, he's getting on at the next stop,' Lisa said raising an eyebrow. 'That's okay, isn't it?'

Davina nodded realising if she made a fuss Lisa may become suspicious and wonder why she was curious about him joining them. 'Yes, of course,' she mumbled. 'The more the merrier and all that.'

Davina wondered if Stewart had a girlfriend, and if so, what she thought about him weekending with five women. She would have loved to ask but didn't want to sound interested then scolded herself for even thinking about the way they'd looked at each other in the lift.

She was a happily married woman, she reminded herself. She was five years older than him and was more than content with her husband. She looked out of the window while the train sped through countryside at the trees and hedges whizzing past. She sighed and wondered why that sounded so hollow and unconvincing.

'God, I've been looking forward to this for months,' Lisa said and told Davina how her parents had arrived the night before to look after the children for two days. 'Drink, food, shopping, and dancing, who could ask for anything more!' She practically squealed.

Davina smiled thinking of Lisa's home life and not for the first time wondered how she managed to fit in everything. She berated herself for feeling tired because she worked full time and hadn't been looking forward to the weekend away Lisa also worked just as many hours but was bringing up three children at the same time.

She sat up further in her seat determined to do her best and make sure Lisa had a great weekend away from washing, ironing, and feeding her brood.

Davina smiled fondly at Lisa and noticed how her black curly hair looked shinier than usual. And, how her eyes danced with excitement. She said, 'You've had your hair done! I thought there was something different when I saw you at the station, it looks lovely.'

Lisa grinned and they chatted about the shops they were looking forward to seeing then turned in their seats to include the others who laughed and shouted in excitement.

The train slowed down to pull into the next station and Lisa called, 'There he is!' She climbed up onto her knees in the seat waving wildly through the window at Stewart.

He spotted her and grinned then hurried along the platform to the carriage door. The girls hooted and giggled when he sauntered down the aisle whistling the tune, I'm getting married in the morning. He sat down in the seat across the aisle from them.

Davina hadn't realised how popular he was amongst the rest of the staff on the ward and felt a little like an outsider. She'd once been the main lynch pin on the ward looking after her nurse's well-being and had known all their home lives and family stories. But now, having taken the leap up to senior management she felt out of touch.

'Morning, boss,' Stewart said cheerfully.

She gave him a friendly smile. 'It's Davina when we're out of work,' she said trying not to sound pompous. To which, all the girls cooed, 'Ooohhhh,'

Davina felt her face flush and knew she would be blushing scarlet. She looked down at her hand twirling her rings around her finger.

Lisa snapped at the girls. 'Cut it out, Davina is old school like me, so a laugh and joke is fine, but just remember you have to face us both again on Monday morning,' she said. 'And we are the ones who dish out the horrible jobs!'

The girls cheered and laughed good-humouredly then began to regale each other with hilarious stories from the ward.

Davina squeezed Lisa's knee in thanks and pulled her shoulders back. She knew a manager's job had to have a certain amount of distance between them but, she thought wistfully, she did miss the camaraderie.

Stewart produced a bottle of champagne from his holdall. 'Hope it's not too early for a taster?' he asked laughing.

Lisa cheered and ran along to the buffet car returning with plastic cups.

Chapter Eight

The two-hour journey, changing trains in Chesterfield, flew over and once they'd checked into the hotel rooms, they all declared themselves ready for shopping. The younger nurses decided to split up and visit New Look, Primark, and the trendy boutique's while Davina and Lisa headed for more select shops.

Davina thought Stewart would have gone with the others, but he insisted upon tagging along with.

'I'm looking for birthday presents for my older twin sisters to post down to London,' he said.

Lisa accepted the shopping challenge and they headed into Debenhams.

Davina soon relaxed and found herself enjoying their company. Jewellery, handbags, and shoes were bought and by lunch time when they piled into a café, she was ravenous. Lisa went to the counter with their orders, and she sat facing Stewart. His loud, boisterous manner had tempered during the morning, and she appreciated the quieter more composed side of his personality.

'My sisters will love the jewellery you've chosen,' he said grinning. 'It shows great taste.'

She looked at his wide twitching mouth. Was he laughing at her or was it a genuine compliment? She said, 'You're making fun of me?'

Suddenly he leant forward resting his elbows on the table. The short sleeves on a black T-shirt stretched tight across his large biceps. 'God, no! I would never do that,' he said drawing bushy eyebrows together. 'I think you're amazing!'

She figured coming from him, this was a genuine compliment and relaxed back into her seat. She chuckled softly. 'Oh, my. I'm that good, eh?'

He smirked. 'Well, I happen to think so. And, when I'm joking and teasing, I don't mean it in a personal way,' he said. 'It's just when I don't know what to say I make a joke. I've found it helps especially when I'm working with a lot of women. Sometimes it's not easy being the only male on the ward.'

Hmm, she mused, maybe all this charm was a screen to hide the fact that he too felt a little insecure. And, she thought seriously, she'd never given his position amongst the twenty female nurses any forethought. Perhaps she wasn't the only one trying to fit in this weekend.

'I can see how that might be difficult,' she said sitting forward until her face was close to his. 'And, if you have any problems with the younger ones please come and talk to me.'

'Oh, I will, I love talking to you, Davina,' he said. 'Just hearing your name makes me quiver.'

Their eyes locked into each other. She felt he was staring right into her heart and soul. Once again, she was transfixed, and her heart began to thump with excitement. She hadn't been certain that day in the lift if she'd imagined the attraction between them but now, she knew for certain. He felt it too.

His eyes softened and widened. She was sure she heard him sigh in pleasure then watched him swallow hard while she licked her dry lips.

'Heavens, what a queue!' Lisa moaned and banged the tray onto the table.

Stewart and Davina sprang apart and looked up at Lisa while she complained about the slow service. Davina stood up quickly and helped her lift the sandwiches and coffee mugs from the tray onto the table.

Lisa looked from Stewart to Davina's face. 'What's up? You both look serious?'

Stewart breezed easily. 'Us? We are never serious. We're having a wonderful time and I was just saying how much my sisters would love their presents.'

Davina smiled her thanks at him for covering over what could have been an awkward situation and he winked cheekily at her.

Really, she thought, he was the limit. His loud, raucous laugh was very infectious and the more time she spent with him the more she liked him. Munching into her sandwich she could hear a voice in the back of her mind. It was her mother's voice with one of her old sayings, you're playing with fire, my, girl.

***

Standing in front of the full-length mirror in her hotel room she swung from side to side looking at the dress she'd brought to wear. She bit her lip worrying that she would look out of place in the night club. But, she reasoned, living in the village meant cosy nights in the local pub or restaurant with Michael. Therefore, her wardrobe was sadly lacking in appropriate dancing clothes.

The dress was plain black crepe in a sleeveless classic style which fitted her figure perfectly. Even the two-inch length above her knee was ideal. She sat on the end of the bed making sure that although it showed off her slim, tanned legs it didn't make her look like a tart in a mini dress.

Yes, she decided, it was simple, yet chic, and was just the thing to stay cool while she danced. She stood up again, smoothed her hands over her hips and for a moment saw herself how she hoped Stewart would see her. A small chest with a tiny waist and long shapely legs. She grabbed her clutch bag, pushed her feet into black patent heels and ran from the room along the corridor to the bar where they were all meeting for cocktails.

Lisa wore red sparkling trousers and a silver top which was low enough to display large mounds of quivering flesh. 'I bought the new outfit especially for this weekend,' she said clinging onto Stewart's arm.

He'd ditched the jeans and T-shirt for black dress trousers and a light grey shirt and although he was only five foot seven, along with his broad chest and chunky shoulders they gave him quite a manly stance.

Stewart untangled himself from Lisa's arm to get Davina a cocktail and they made their way into the hotel restaurant. She sat in between Lisa and Stewart at a round table and could feel Stewart's eyes boring into her side while she sipped the cocktail.

One of the younger nurses mentioned a shop they'd been into which had Christmas cards at the checkout, and Lisa moaned. 'Oh, no, don't even go there!'

With the effects of the cocktail loosening her shoulders Davina joined in the conversation. 'I know it's far too early to think about Christmas, the shops get earlier every year.'

Stewart smiled. 'Well, this year I've got to be one of the early shoppers because my parents have moved out to Spain to live so I'll have to be organised to send their gifts in the post. And although I'm going to visit, we're not flying until Boxing Day morning.'

Davina listened avidly to this piece of information deciding the words, we are, sounded as though he wasn't alone in his Christmas plans.

He turned to face her. 'So, what do you get up to at Christmas, Davina,' he asked quietly.

She looked down at his thick fingers and the roughened skin around his nails.

'Oh, we do the same things every year,' she said. 'We have both sets of parents over and the traditional turkey, old fashioned cards, a real tree with the same baubles and decorations. Then we watch the same TV programs and the Queen's speech.'

Lisa squinted and sighed heavily. 'But what do you want to do, Davina?'

She could hear the terseness in Lisa's voice but ignored it. 'Well, just trivial things really. To be honest, I'm not that keen on turkey, and I'd love to cook a whole salmon. And last year we received snazzy Christmas cards from Australia that were done on a computer. I'd love to try them,' she said wistfully. 'Or maybe jet off somewhere hot for New Years to party on the beach!'

She could see envy glowering in Lisa's eyes. She knew her friend was wondering how she could be unsatisfied with her perfect Christmas and everything she shared with Michael. But Davina wanted to scream at her. Yes, she had everything except the one thing she couldn't have and that was a baby. She wanted to tell her how she longed to watch her own kids opening their stockings and presents on Christmas morning. But instead, she swallowed hard, took a deep breath, and smiled at everyone around the table.

Stewart nodded. 'Well, I've never had the same routines every year, not even as a child, because my father was in the army and we moved location every few years,' he said smiling. 'But at the same time, I can see how it would get monotonous and being a spontaneous type of guy, I'd soon be longing for change.'

She smiled at him draining her cocktail, knowing in his way that he was siding with her and understood how she felt.

'Now, who's for red and white wine?' Lisa asked while they read the menus.

The restaurant in the hotel only held seven round tables and for a weekend night it wasn't busy. Davina looked around at the trendy décor in black and white but decided it felt cold and lacked any type of warmth and atmosphere. And she sighed; looking at the prices on the menu she knew it was not what the nurses would call reasonable.

She took £100 out of her purse and placed it firmly in the middle of the table. 'This money was given to me from a patient's relatives with strict instructions that it was for the nurses to enjoy themselves,' she said looking at their happy faces. 'So, because everyone is having a fun time, I think we should spend it now.'

Whoops of laughter and thanks were called out, and Stewart ordered two bottles of Chardonnay and Cabernet.

When the waiter hovered behind Davina to pour wine into her glass, she felt torn. She knew the cocktail contained the limit of alcohol she usually allowed herself, but Cabernet was her favourite and would be lovely with the steak she'd ordered.

Since the day her and Michael had left the infertility clinic two years ago, they had made a pact with each other to limit themselves to two glasses of alcohol. There'd been occasions when Michael had wanted more, and she'd stopped him and, vice versa, but she thought shifting uneasily in her chair, he'd never know if she overstepped the mark tonight.

'Go, on,' Stewart whispered in her ear. 'It'll do you the world of good. Relax, unwind and go with the flow.'

She felt the heat from his sleeve when he leaned close to her while the waiter poured wine into his glass at his right side. She wanted to, in fact, she wanted nothing more, but Stewart didn't know about the fertility regime and what the consequences could be. She looked up at the waiter and slowly nodded. 'Cabernet, please.'

Lisa squeezed her hand. 'It can't make that much difference, honey, not for one night,' she soothed.

Davina shrugged her shoulders. 'You're right. Well, nothing is happening anyway whatever I do, so ca sera.'

Stewart looked puzzled while Davina took two large mouthfuls of wine and tucked into her steak. Her shoulders relaxed as she felt the alcohol flow through her veins and sighed softly in contentment. That's so good, she mused, listening to everyone's chatter and felt her mood lift.

Chapter Nine

Shortly before eleven they all trooped single file past the door attendants outside the nearby nightclub and down a flight of stairs into a large dark room. Davina adjusted her eyes in the darkness while she helped Lisa safely down the last two steps onto a carpet that felt sticky under her shoes.

The square room with a large dance floor in the middle had seen better days, Davina thought, but it didn't matter because she was enjoying herself so much. She had stopped counting after her third glass of wine and now declared to Lisa, that she felt quite drunk.

'It's great to see you so happy and enjoying yourself,' Lisa slurred.

The hen, followed by the nurses and balloons formed a conga chain to dance their way across the floor towards two empty tables in the corner of the club.

She put her hands onto Lisa's waist shouting, 'Come- on, join-up!'

Davina began to jiggle her legs out copying the girls in front. Suddenly, she gasped feeling Stewart's big hands gripping her slim hips. His hot breath was behind her ear while he followed her across the room laughing and shouting. She could feel the heat from his touch through the thin crepe material and felt ripples of excitement flood through her body.

Leaving their bags under the table they all ran onto the dance floor and were immediately lost amongst the crowds of sweating young bodies jumping and dancing. Davina didn't know much of the up-to-date songs but danced and laughed while the loud music pulsated in ears.

By one in the morning and after numerous gin and tonic's, Davina's head was swimming. The nurses had left to go back to the hotel, and she found herself alone with Stewart on the dance floor. The music changed from a fast upbeat tempo to a slow love song, and he pulled her towards him.

'If you don't want this, now is the time to say and we can follow the others back to the hotel,' he whispered into her ear. 'I'm drunk and don't want to stop but if you do then that's what we'll do.'

She threw her head back in complete abandonment. She knew she should break away from him and return to the hotel like sensible Mrs Davina Philips would do. She should remove her make-up, text her husband goodnight, and climb into bed with a clear conscience. But she didn't want to do that.

The room was spinning and although she knew she was very drunk she didn't want the night to end. She felt wonderful, totally carefree and was having the time of her life. She was fed up with playing the married woman who everyone felt sorry for because she couldn't get pregnant.

Here, at this moment with Stewart there were no constrictions, no regimes to follow, and nothing planned to within an inch of its life. It was simply pure enjoyment and fun. She snaked her arms around his neck. He pulled her up against him and she heard him groan with pleasure.

'You're gorgeous,' he breathed into her ear. 'I've wanted to be close to you since the first time I saw you.'

While she snuggled her face into his neck, Davina could smell the spicy remains of his aftershave mixed with manly sweat. He began to slide his big hands up and down her spine which made her tingle with desire.

'Let's get out of here,' she whispered in his ear.

They ran out of the club into the dark night air, and he stopped at the corner wall of an alleyway to steady himself. 'Wow! The fresh air has knocked the wind out of me,' he said placing a hand on the wall.

She stared at his thick lips and wondered what they would taste like? Only one way to find out, she mused and throwing aside the little amount of decorum she had left, she grabbed his hand, pulled him into the alley and kissed him.

The look of delighted surprise flooded his face. He put both his arms around her waist and pulled her into him. His lips devoured her mouth roughly and she felt like she was being sucked into him. She wanted him so much that she felt almost lightheaded with lust. They broke away from each other and hurried along the road into the hotel.

The bright lights in the hotel reception made her blink and her heels clicked loudly on the tiled floor. She let go of his hand and took them off.

'My room or yours?'

He breathed heavily fumbling in his pocket for the key-card. Frantically, she tried to remember if Lisa was in the next room to her.

'Yours,' she cried running down the corridor with him.

Davina nearly fell into the room behind him and knew this was going to be pure unbridled sex. She intended to enjoy every minute. Just for one night she was going to do what she wanted. Not what was expected of her or what other people wanted. It wasn't making love to conceive babies but simply an act to fulfil a need. She found the freedom exhilarating.

He flicked on the bedside lamp, but she reached up the wall and turned on the main lights. 'I want to see you,' she stated. 'And I don't want this to be safely on a bed in the dark.'

He nodded looking at her with oval eyes that widened. 'Anything, Davina,' he whispered. 'Just say what you want, and I'll do it!'

Slowly she pulled her black dress up over head and threw it to the floor. 'I want to enjoy sex again. I don't want to think about anything else. I just want to do it for pure pleasure alone,' she said staring brazenly at him. 'Can you understand that?'

He nodded slowly unzipping his trousers and letting them fall from his legs. 'Yeah, I get that,' he said and stepped out of them in red stripy boxer shorts.

He shrugged his shoulders. 'Hay, if I'd known this was going to happen tonight, I'd have worn my best.'

She giggled then laughed. It felt so good to laugh again that she wanted to cry and scream and love every minute of being an attractive woman.

'Do you want another drink?' he asked unbuttoning his shirt.

'No, I can't wait that long. I'm sick of waiting for the right time and place. I want you now,' she said and flung herself towards him.

He held her at bay with strong powerful arms. He had a tattoo on his left arm with the name, Chloe, and she traced it with her finger wondering who she was.

'Do you think I'm sexy, Stewart?' she asked.

He leered at her black lace bra and then slid a finger into the side of her black hipster pants and pulled her towards him. 'You're kidding, right?' he groaned. 'Davina, you ooze sex appeal no matter where you are and whatever you're doing. Even at work in a serious situation I could rip the clothes from you!'

She put both her hands onto his broad chest which was thick with brown hair and moaned softly.

His lips devoured her mouth, and she felt her legs wobble as every nerve in her body cried out for him. The more excited he became the wider he opened his mouth and she groaned in ecstasy. She felt as if he was sucking the very life out of her. She pulled his shorts down and he threw his head back then howled like an animal in pain.

He put his hands into her hair and scrunched it into handfuls. 'Oh, Davina. I've prayed for this since that day in the lift.'

'Please, please, don't talk anymore,' she gabbled breathing hard. 'Don't make me wait any longer. I need you now!'

He bent down then flung her backwards onto the settee and climbed on top of her. She cried out in ecstasy and wrapped her legs around his broad back to match his rhythm. She begged for more and felt the climax explode inside her when he collapsed spent on top of her.

Chapter Ten

Michael sat in the lounge waiting for Davina to come downstairs. She'd practically ran upstairs when they'd got back from the train station telling him she needed to unpack and take a shower.

Davina had hardly spoken a word in the car on the journey home and looked absolutely wrecked. He turned the sound low on the TV because the sound of football commentary usually irritated her. After waiting an hour, he went upstairs to find her in bed asleep. An empty foil packet of painkillers lay on the bedside table with a glass of water. Wearily he rolled into bed next to her.

At seven the next morning he spooned her back wondering why she was wearing a long nightshirt. 'Happy birthday, sweetheart,' he crooned into her ear.

She jerked awake then groaned softly. 'Jeez, it can't be that time already?'

He smiled and cuddled her close inhaling her natural sleepy smell. 'I'm afraid so.'

Automatically, she threw the quilt aside and got up padding slowly into the en suite.

He called, 'Hey, what's with the night shirt?'

She put her head around the door. 'Oh, I felt chilly last night. I'm sorry I didn't come back downstairs my head was thumping.'

'That's okay,' he said pleased that she seemed to be in a better mood. 'Do you want your birthday gift now or do you want to wait until we get home from work?'

'Later,' she mumbled through a mouthful of toothpaste.

He got up and went into the bathroom to shower but when he came back into the bedroom she'd climbed back into bed and was lying facing the wall.

'I'm going to phone in sick,' she mumbled from under the quilt. 'I feel rotten. My heads still aching, and I feel sick.'

He stopped in his tracks. In all the years they'd been together he'd never once known her stay off work. In fact, even when she had been poorly, she'd dragged herself into the hospital not wanting to let her patients down.

He frowned. 'Okay, rest up today and hopefully you'll be feeling better for tonight. Your mum has booked us a table at an Indian restaurant on the Golden Mile.'

She groaned. 'I'll ring them later.'

Michael kissed the top of her head and stroked her hair. 'I'll ring around lunch time to see how you're feeling,' he said hurrying from the bedroom.

***

When Michael reached their office, he wandered through the door to see Stella sitting in his chair swinging her legs in a short black skirt.

'Ah, here he is,' she said smiling. 'I was just asking Anthony if you were in today.'

He hung his black jacket on the peg behind the door and looked at Anthony wondering if he'd forgotten something. Usually, the only time they had contact with the production managers was if they were due to work in the factory.

But Anthony gave a reassuring nod. 'Stella wondered if she could have the recipe for the new stuffing, we tasted last week. She's thinking of making it at home this weekend for a dinner party.'

Michael smiled and perched himself on the edge of the desk. She made to get up and give him his chair back, but he motioned for her to stay where she was. 'So, are you cooking turkey?'

She shook her curls. 'No, but I'm thinking of maybe a ham joint or chicken breasts,' she said smiling up at him. 'Do you think it would work the same?'

'Hmm, I'm not too sure about the ham because it's already got smoked pancetta in the recipe. Although, you could take that out?'

Anthony interrupted. 'Look, why don't you go through the recipe with Stella while I make us all a coffee,' he said. 'Milk and sugar, Stella?'

'No sugar, I'm sweet enough,' she said giggling.

Michael noticed she wrinkled her small button nose when she laughed and couldn't help but warm to her. She had such a friendly manner. 'So, you like to cook?' he asked.

'Well, I don't bother much when I'm on my own,' she said. 'But I do like to make an effort when I have friends over. And that is what this dinner party is all about. With being new to the area, I've invited three neighbouring couples to dinner hoping to socialise a little more.'

They discussed the merits of cooking meals from scratch as opposed to ready meals while Anthony placed coffee mugs down in front of them.

Anthony asked, 'And where does your husband work?'

She looked down at her bare fourth finger and her cheeks flushed. 'Oh, I'm divorced now. I have been for a few years. My son, Simon is away at university in Edinburgh studying medicine. He wants to be a doctor.'

Michael glowered at Tony. It still amazed him after all the years he'd known him how tactless he could be in conversation. He had obviously embarrassed her by asking directly about her husband. He decided to move the subject on to her son. 'A doctor, eh? You must be proud of him?'

Her shoulders relaxed and she grinned. 'Oh, yes. I am. He's doing very well in his studies but it's going to be a long hard slog.'

Michael sipped his coffee. 'Yeah, I've heard it's a five-year degree?'

He often daydreamed about the son he and Davina would have and how he could steer him into great professions like medicine or law. He'd had such high hopes of their family, but wondered now, if they would only be dreams.

'You must miss him?' Anthony asked. 'It's a fair trek up to Scotland from here.'

She nodded and her gentle eyes dulled behind the glasses. 'It is but I'm glad that he's a long distance from here, it's safer that way.'

Anthony put his head on one side and Michael could tell he was going to probe further, so he ruffled under the pile of papers on his desk to distract them. 'Now, I know the recipe is here somewhere,' he said smiling at her.

She shook her shoulders slightly as if she were casting aside unwelcome memories and muttered, 'Thanks, Michael.'

Triumphantly, he pulled a piece of paper from the bottom.

'Ta Dah,' he said smoothing the crumples out on the desk surface. 'Now, I'm sure fennel is like fat bulbous celery with the same crunchy texture. But it does have a marked aniseed flavour which I reckon would go well with fish. How about trout? Or you could use it in a pasta dish?'

Stella frowned. 'Hmm, I've already checked with my guests and one of them has coeliac disease, so pasta is out.'

'Right,' he said nodding and thought about different meat varieties. 'Well, how about a pork joint? You could buy one from here and get the butchers to debone and roll it for you.'

'Wow!' she exclaimed grinning. 'That's a great idea! I knew you'd come up with something. I could tell the moment I met you that you were a guy who'd have all the answers to life's problems.'

Michael knew she was teasing him again and where previously he'd felt embarrassed by the one-to-one attention, now he was enjoying it. She was fun to be around, he decided and seriously cute into the bargain. 'Well, I wouldn't say that, and I'm not a chef, but I do know a lot about meat.'

'A lot?' Anthony chortled. 'He knows everything there is to know about meat joints and the best accompaniments. Afterall, I've been teaching him for years!'

Michael raised his eyebrows and tutted at Anthony while Stella giggled at their duo act.

'Look,' Michael said sliding off the desk while she drained her coffee. 'Why not call in later this afternoon with the pork joint and we'll make the recipe in the kitchen then stuff it.'

She looked up at him and burst out laughing. 'So, I've to come back later to get stuffed?'

'Why not!' He cried and laughed with her. 'See you around two?'

When Stella had left the office Anthony started typing an email. 'Be careful there, Michael,' he warned. 'She really fancies you and I know you've not had a good time at home lately, but this could be dodgy.'

Michael grunted and puffed while he booted up his computer then sat down in his chair. What rubbish, he thought, as if he would even think about cheating on Davina. But the chair was still warm from where Stella had sat, and he just caught the remains of her light flowery perfume. It made him wriggle with stirrings of desire.

After lunch and with paperwork finished, he headed into the kitchen to prepare the ingredients for Stella. While he lifted out bags of breadcrumb, sage, and garlic puree from the freezer he couldn't help but wonder what she'd meant by her son being safely tucked away up in Scotland. However, it would have to remain a mystery because he prided himself upon being tactful and wouldn't dream of upsetting her again by asking. If she ventured information that would be fine but if not, then it wasn't any of his business.

Anthony had returned from a management meeting just before lunch where he'd heard the operations manager singing Stella's praises. The entire site was impressed with her excellent organisational skills and hardworking ethic. The operators on the shop floor said she was fair, always ready to listen, and understood the challenges they faced every day. In just a short space of time, she had improved manufacturing outputs.

'Boo!' she cried joyfully from behind him.

Startled, he swung around because he hadn't heard her come into the kitchen. 'Oh, hello. I didn't know you were there,' he said.

She closed the door behind her. 'It's the soft flat shoes I wear. They're great for creeping up and shocking people, especially if they're doing something they shouldn't be,' she said looking down at them.

He followed her gaze and ogled the thick black tights on her slim legs disappearing under the short skirt. She turned her back and removed her jacket laying it over the door handle then turned back to face him.

He swallowed hard and just stopped himself from gasping aloud. The blue V-neck, T-shirt she wore was stretched tight across the most voluptuous chest he'd ever seen on such a little woman. They had to be at least three times bigger than Davina's and compared to the rest of her tiny frame they looked huge. He mused; on a taller lady they wouldn't look that big but on her they made her look top heavy. As though she was about to topple over. Michael tried hard not to stare.

He took a deep breath and looked down at the bench trying to get his thoughts in order. Perhaps Anthony was right, and he was in a vulnerable place because he'd give anything right now just to bury his face in her cleavage.

She plonked the pork joint onto the bench and joked. 'It's already for stuffing!'

The laughter in her voice broke his reverie and they began to work together mixing the ingredients and stuffing the pork joint. Conversation flowed easily between them, and he found himself confiding in her about Davina and the fertility clinic.

She told him how she'd been a victim of her abusive husband. How she had ran away from him staying first in a hostel for battered women then eventually building a new life for her and Simon.

'It was the jealousy that used to start the beatings,' she muttered. 'He was obsessed with the fact that I was having an affair behind his back, though God knows why. I never looked at another man. I was crazy about him from the first night we met but he never believed me.'

'And you don't know where he is now?' Michael asked appalled at the thought of any man beating this tiny woman.

She stared down at the pork. 'Still in Surrey, I believe. That's where all my family are and where I had to run from. I knew if I stayed there, he'd never leave us alone and I didn't want that for Simon,' she said. 'He'd seen enough by the age of fourteen. Unfortunately, more than any child should ever see.'

Michael laid his hand on her shoulder. 'You poor little thing,' he soothed. 'I just cannot comprehend why some men think the only way to get what they want from a woman is by using their fists. Not when there's so many other ways.'

'Yeah,' she said brightening and stared up into his eyes. 'And I bet you are a master at all the other ways?'

She was able to jump from sadness to upbeat in seconds but maybe that was the way she'd managed to cope with her situation. He hoped she hadn't thought he was being blasé.

He sighed, 'Well, I used to pride myself in that department but now I'm not sure that Davina would agree. She doesn't seem to want me anywhere near her.'

She touched her throat. 'Really? I can't believe that,' she said then wrapped the joint in tin foil. 'Maybe it's just a phase and she'll snap out of it?'

'I do hope so,' he grumbled clearing the bench.

Chapter Eleven

Davina lay back against the pillows in bed. She had a cold facecloth across her forehead and Michael sat on the end of the bed. She had opened her gifts and cards. Her mum had called earlier full of concern.

'I'm sorry about cancelling tonight, Michael,' she said and averted his eyes. 'I cannot seem to shift this headache and my legs still feel like jelly.'

Her face was flushed, and he could tell by the way she rubbed her nose and ears that she was agitated. The bedroom was warm with the central heating turned on high and he unbuttoned the neck of his shirt. 'Are you sure you don't want me to call the doctor?'

'Nooo, it's probably just flu. Nothing to worry about, there's loads of people at work got it. I could have picked it up from someone at the weekend,' she gabbled then bit her lip. 'I mean, well no one seemed to have flu, but you never know.'

He stared at her and frowned. 'Okay, I'll go and get myself something to eat then come back up later to see how you are,' he said firmly. 'But if you're no better tomorrow I'm definitely calling the doctor.'

When he crawled into bed that night, she lay facing the wall away from him. He wrapped his arms around and felt her stiffen then inch away from him. Was there something else other than the flu, he wondered then tried to get her to talk about Leeds. But she clammed up ignoring his questions.

He ran his hand through her hair, 'Come on, love,' he whispered and licked the side of ear. 'Just talk to me.' But she pushed him away in what he felt was a rough manner.

She shouted, 'For God's sake! Can you not leave me alone? I'm ill and you're still pawing at me because it's the fertile week. Surely to God I can have one blooming week off!'

He bristled at her rejection. 'I wasn't pawing at you to make love,' he shouted. 'And I can see you are poorly I was simply trying to get you to tell me what's wrong!'

'Look, there's nothing to talk about,' she sighed heavily. 'Now please sleep on your side of the bed and let me be.'

He flung himself across the other side of the bed groaning miserably and stared up at the white ceiling. His stomach churned at how she'd spoken to him and the words she had used. No matter how many times she told him nothing was wrong, he knew better. There was certainly something sadly amiss.

***

By the end of November Davina was in despair. She knew she was pregnant. It was nine weeks since she'd had a period but didn't need to look at the horrid calendar. She had felt different since the week after Leeds.

The day before she had gone to the chemist and picked up a pregnancy testing kit but had put it back on the shelf knowing it would only tell her what she already knew. When she'd got outside onto the street, she had been in tears remembering how in the past, she had longed to see the little blue line.

Sitting in her office she stared miserably at the computer screen. She thought how laughable it would be if it wasn't so sad. She hadn't told anyone about the baby mainly because she still didn't know for absolute certain who the father was. Every time she thought about Leeds her face flushed and she felt physically sick with shame.

It had been the pain in her forehead that had woken her at six the following morning in Stewart's hotel bedroom. At first, she hadn't grasped where she was until she'd opened her eyes and stared at his hairy broad back facing away from her. The headache had been thunderous and when she'd remembered what she had done bile gathered in the back of her throat. The thought of vomiting in his bed, which would have added further shame to her lewd behaviour, made her crawl quietly out from under the duvet. She had gathered her clothes, hurriedly dressed in the bathroom, and staggered along the corridor to her own room.

Davina had heard the gentle click of a door and thought for one horrible moment that he'd followed her. But when she'd looked over her shoulder no one had been there. She had tried twice to scrub the smell of him from her body in the shower crying all the while then sent a text.

'Stewart, it's all been a terrible mistake. I don't want to see you again, and I hope you can forgive me, Davina.'

Shaking the foul memories from her mind she stared at the unwritten report and wondered, not for the first time that week, what actual use she was at work. She couldn't think about anything else but the baby and on more than one occasion had fretted herself into a state of near hysteria.

A tear rolled down her cheek as she stared at an untouched mug of coffee on the desk because the smell made her stomach retch which she knew was morning sickness. If only she could turn the clock back nine weeks. She would never have gone to Leeds and could be certain that it was Michael's baby.

But, she thought miserably, that would never happen because she'd behaved like a trollop and had no one else to blame but herself for the shameful situation. She certainly couldn't find any happiness in the fact that she was pregnant. She had lain next to Michael in bed for weeks riddled with guilt and could still barely look him in the eye. So, how would she tell him that she was pregnant with another man's child?

In lighter moments she tried to reason that it still could be Michaels because they had made love in Turkey the night before they flew home. The sex in Leeds hadn't happened until the following weekend. But this thought made her more desolate to think that she could have been pregnant when she'd been with Stewart.

She packed her briefcase for the day and decided to go home early then try to come to a decision. She knew she would have to take action soon because although she was wearing loose clothing and nightshirts to hide the small mound in her belly she would soon start to show.

***

When she left the ward, the sounds and smells of the busy orthopaedic ward wafted towards her. A patient was being pushed down the corridor towards theatre by the newly married hen and two of the junior nurses were standing talking to one of the medical team. She knew the dressings were being done in the treatment room because she could smell the strong smell of Betadine antiseptic solution.

Just when she turned the corner towards the lift Stewart swaggered towards her in his white tunic and black trousers. From the day they'd returned to work after the Leeds fiasco he'd practically ignored her. For which she'd been truly grateful. But now, she could tell by the smirk on his face that he didn't intend to pass by without saying something.

Anxiously she glanced around and breathed a sigh of relief. The corridor and lift area were empty. Her heart raced in trepidation. Please don't make a scene, she thought, because she couldn't take much more.

'You look knackered?' he said gently.

She smiled. 'I am. I'm going to take this report home to work on,' she said and took a deep breath. The smell of his aftershave, which she'd thought manly in Leeds, now made her want to retch. She swallowed hard.

He stared into her eyes as if searching for an answer. 'We've never really talked since the weekend away,' he said. 'But I just wanted to say I've never regretted it, not once.'

She shook her head, bit down on her bottom lip, and looked past him towards her route of escape. 'None of this has anything to do with you, Stewart, it's totally my fault. I was very drunk and screwed up at the time,' she said taking another deep breath to keep the sickness at bay. 'And I'm truly ashamed of myself. It was nothing you did or didn't do and I'm deeply sorry.'

He laughed softly. 'I was going to say I thought you were magnificent and if ever you change your mind or want to give it another whirl you know where I am.'

She nodded and sighed with relief. 'Okay, but that won't happen. Sorry, I have to go,' she said and walked purposively towards the lifts.

When she pressed the button the lift doors pinged open, and she stepped inside nearly crying with release. The doors closed and she leant her hot cheeks against the cold stainless-steel wall.

He'd been the perfect gentleman about their affair, and she knew a lesser man might have been bitter towards her. He would have been within his rights to verbally abuse her following the abrupt brush off by text.

Therefore, surely this man, as did any other man, would have the right to know he was going to be a father? Would he be pleased? Or would he be appalled at the thought of having a child.

If she knew his feelings towards the pregnancy were the latter, then she could be certain that he wouldn't want any interaction with the baby. She sighed and wondered if she could get away with telling Michael the baby was his and avoid hurting him. He need never know any different.

Chapter Twelve

When she arrived home, she walked slowly through the lounge and dropped her briefcase onto the leather armchair. It was Michael's chair, or the chair Michael always sat in to watch TV. She trailed her hand along the back where the leather felt different and was slightly worn from the shape of his head.

She thought of him and sighed. He was a good man and deserved to know the truth about the baby. But she also knew the truth would devastate him and she would have his ruin on her conscience forevermore. When she thought of living alone for the rest of her life because she knew he would never consent to bring up another man's child, it loomed like a big black cloud.

Davina lay down on the settee and put her head on a soft cushion. She felt alone and wrapped in her own bubble with no one to talk to about the baby. She wished she hadn't lost touch with her best friend, Jane.

After all their childhood spent together Jane and her family had emigrated to Australia. At the age of sixteen they'd sworn to keep in touch, but inevitably they'd grown apart and now were only Christmas and birthday card friends.

Michael, whom she'd met at seventeen had soon taken over Jane's place as her best friend. She closed her heavy eyelids and decided that deep inside her she knew it couldn't possibly be Michael's baby as much as she wished it was. After all their barren years together, it simply had to be Stewart's. Her eyes stung with tiredness and just before she dozed off, she wondered if it would be unjust not to tell Stewart that he was a father.

***

The next morning, she sat opposite a GP in her local surgery. She'd made the appointment to get a sick note because she felt too tired to go into work and hoped a few weeks at home would give her time to make the decision. Her usual GP was on holiday, so her appointment was with a locum, Doctor Evans, who thankfully was female.

While the doctor read her notes on a computer screen, Davina looked around the small consulting room at the promotional good health posters.

Doctor Evans looked up at her. 'So, Davina. What can I do for you?'

'Well, I think I'm at least nine weeks pregnant and feel exhausted,' she said. 'I had to come home from work yesterday because I couldn't keep my eyes open. And I wondered if I could have a sick note to rest up for a while?'

The grey-haired doctor, who Davina judged to be in her late fifties, sat back in the chair and drew her bushy eyebrows together. 'Hmm, you don't look happy to be pregnant,' she muttered. 'I can see by your records the fertility problems you've had and would have thought you'd be dancing around the room or at least be smiling.'

Davina felt the avalanche of tears spill out of her and felt too weary to hold them back. In between sobs she blurted out the whole story and sat with her head bent. The tears ran down her cheeks and dropped onto her black leather handbag which she clutched firmly on her lap.

'Oh, dear,' Doctor Evans soothed with kindness in her eyes. 'What a pickle to be in.'

She moved the box of tissues across the desk to Davina who lifted her head and dried her wet face but still couldn't stop sobbing.

Doctor Evans wore a pale blue jumper which matched her eyes and had a motherly rosy-cheeked face. She smiled at Davina reassuringly. 'Look, let's get you checked over physically first and make sure this little nipper is okay, then we'll talk through the rest?'

Davina sighed with relief. For the first time in weeks, she didn't feel alone. She had spoken the words aloud and someone else was making the decisions about what to do. They were only small decisions about the here and now. She also knew the doctor wouldn't tell her what to do long term, but it was a start. She blew her nose, followed her behind the screen, and lay back on the couch.

'Well, everything seems fine in there, Davina. We'll get you booked for a scan and set the ball in motion for antenatal classes.'

While Doctor Evans washed her hands in the sink, Davina pulled on her jeans thinking about the baby, or the nipper, as doctor had called it. She emerged from behind the screen and sat back down on the chair.

Doctor Evans began to type on the keypad. 'Er, and when did this slight indiscretion take place?'

Davina smiled at her choice of words deciding they sounded much kinder than drunken sex with a colleague in a hotel room. She told her the date and the day in Turkey with Michael.

Davina asked, 'So, because Michael and I haven't been able to conceive for over seven years it's got to be Stewarts, hasn't it?'

The older woman rested her thin fingers on the cushioned pad in the front of her keyboard. 'Well, I'm not sure if you know this but DNA testing is considered dangerous for the unborn baby,' she stated resolutely. 'So, you're going to have to wait until after the birth to determine who is the father. But, in all my thirty years sitting here opposite pregnant ladies I can only say nothing in life surprises me now.'

Davina nodded solemnly. 'But you think it's more likely not to be my husbands?'

Doctor Evans smiled. 'I suppose if I were a gambler, I'd put my money on Stewart but there's always what's called an outside chance.'

Davina left the surgery feeling happier than when she'd arrived and stepped out into a cold but sunny afternoon. She was still in the same situation but felt enormously relieved after talking about it to someone, especially someone who hadn't judged her. She had done enough of that herself.

Setting off to walk home she picked up her pace feeling more positive. After all, she reasoned, hadn't the doctor told her she wasn't the first woman in the world to make a mistake. And at least the baby was okay. Which, even though she didn't feel happy to be pregnant, she knew it was her job to protect and nurture.

Doctor Evans had been supportive and kind insisting this reaction was understandable in the circumstances and had comforted her with the fact that she would soon feel differently towards, the little nipper.

The scan would be in four weeks' time and when she turned from the village shops to walk up Greengate Lane, she knew she would have to tell Michael soon.

She walked slowly towards the corner of Hallam Fields Road loving the sight of their smart town house. From their first viewing she'd known it was the right house for them but now she sighed. When Michael knew the truth and he left her, what would happen to the house?

They'd saved since the day they were married to be able to move out of a crummy ground floor flat and into Birstall village. It had been their dream location. Michael's parents lived in the nearby village of Wanlip, and everyone had agreed Birstall would be the ideal place to raise their children.

***

When she put her key in the door Lisa rang. She hurried up the stairs balancing the mobile between her ear and shoulder. She explained about the tiredness and sick note for two weeks and Lisa commiserated.

'I'm just exhausted and feeling a little down,' Davina told her. 'And the doctor has taken blood tests just to rule out anaemia and told me to rest up.'

'Hmm, well make sure you do that,' Lisa nagged but Davina imagined the look of genuine concern there would be on her face.

She poured herself a glass of cold water at the kitchen sink and asked, 'Is everything okay on the ward?'

'Well, there's only one major piece of news,' Lisa gabbled. 'Stewart has handed in his notice! Apparently, he's got a charge nurse job in a hospital down in Bournemouth and he finishes on Christmas Eve.'

Davina could hear the mixture of excited gossip in Lisa's voice tinged with sadness because he was leaving.

She ended the call and sank down onto the settee greedily gulping at the water because her mouth was dry. Oh, halleluiah, she breathed deeply. This was fantastic news because it meant he would be hundreds of miles away and would not see her bump growing month by month. In fact, she decided, if she didn't tell anyone at work, he wouldn't even know she was pregnant before he left the area.

Plus, she thought logically, even when she told him about the baby if he did want fathers' rights, he would not be able to call regularly because of the distance. It could only be once a fortnight or monthly visits? Or, she thought, in seven months' time, after the birth, if the DNA test confirmed that the baby was his, did she really have to tell him at all?

Tucking her legs up on the settee she determined not to think about Stewart anymore until next July. She would make her mind up then and not before. But now, she thought, chewing her bottom lip she had to concentrate on Michael.

Chapter Thirteen

By the last day of November, Michael and Anthony were working long days to get through all the trials they needed for Christmas turkey roasts. The information and testing data from the samples was their responsibility, and Anthony often said, everything should be ready well before launch day when the roasts would go out to the supermarkets.

Michael inhaled the fresh meat aroma while watching three burly butchers layer the turkey, guinea fowl, and duck. They worked at two tables deboning breast meat from each bird and tying them together.

In a quiet voice, Anthony asked Michael, 'Are things any better at home?'

Michael bent over a stainless-steel table and began to write details on labels. He looked at Anthony thinking about his question. 'Not really, about the same. I suppose the atmosphere is pleasant and cordial but not as husband and wife, if you get my drift?'

Anthony nodded seriously. 'I suppose you being here 24 / 7 isn't helping?'

It was six at night and they'd both been at work since seven that morning. Michael yawned in agreement. 'To be honest,' he muttered. 'I don't think she'd miss me if I didn't go home at night, no matter how late it was.'

The line manager began to run the line and the roasts were placed into square red trays on the conveyor belt. Anthony nodded with satisfaction at the size and perfect fit of the packaging they'd chosen to support the roasts.

Michael smiled and packed the samples into crates. He hadn't expected any problems on the line because they'd ran the same roast last Christmas, but he knew due to experience, it was often the smallest and easiest production run that could throw up an issue at the last minute.

They discussed how the three-bird roast was quickly becoming a modern day classic and Michael wondered if this was the year for change. Perhaps, he could cook one for their parents on Christmas Day? The roasts were perfectly suited to a smaller gathering, feeding six to eight people generously. However, he'd have to find out if everyone liked guinea fowl and duck.

This variety of stuffing had apple and apricot in the recipe. Michael smiled with pleasure at the fruity aroma. He thought of Christmas Day and how they would all be impressed with the full-flavoured turkey, guinea fowl and rich tasting duck meat.

When the trial finished and it was deemed a success, they left the office together and walked out into the chilly night air. Anthony said, 'Are you going to the Christmas party night next week?'

He smiled and nodded. 'Yeah, I'm really looking forward to it. Stella doesn't know where the restaurant is, so I've offered to pick her up in a taxi.'

He could tell Anthony was ready to answer with another reproach about Stella and their friendship. He raised an eyebrow and gave him a look as if to say, it's none of your business. Anthony shrugged his shoulders then climbed into his car.

***

With work behind him, Michael stood under a steaming hot shower deciding what clothes to wear to the Christmas party night. Although Davina had offered to drive him into Leicester he'd refused and had booked a taxi.

He hummed the last tune he'd heard on the car radio and knew this wouldn't be the last time tonight he would hear the words, 'Oh, I wish it could be Christmas every day.' He felt upbeat while he towelled himself dry and chose his dark indigo jeans and black shirt to wear. It was months since he'd had a good night out and the state of his marriage, through no fault of his own, was beginning to drag him down.

When he thought back to the argument that had ensued after her birthday night it still rankled him. He had been outraged when she accused him of pawing her. He'd always thought kissing or licking her ear was a loving gesture but finding out that she thought differently had humiliated him.

He had lain awake for hours and stared at the ceiling in total shock while her words had swum around in his mind. He had felt in such a state that he longed for a cigarette to calm down, but he gave up smoking five years ago. However, in stressful situations he would still crave his old habit.

The following night he'd told her that if she needed a break from making love that was fine, and he wouldn't make any more advances. She'd cried and apologised repeatedly and had tried to reassure him that she hadn't felt pawed at, but he'd put his hand up in front of her face in a warning sign. 'No!' He had stated. 'It's obvious that you're comparing my advances to a dog pawing at you which I find degrading to say the least.' His face had flushed, and the rest of his body had broken out into a cold sweat. 'So, in the future, well, let's just say you'll have to make the first move.'

From that night they'd slept on their respectful sides of the bed. They had begun and ended their days with a simple peck on the cheek. Which, he thought was magnanimous of him because any other man wouldn't have tolerated her behaviour and would have left weeks ago.

But no more, he thought now and ran down the stairs. Tonight, was going to be all about enjoying himself with good wine, food, scintillating conversation, and he might even get Stella onto the dance floor for a Christmas boogie.

Calling to Davina not to wait up, he left the house and climbed into the back of the taxi.

***

Stella's shining copper curls seemed to sparkle under the bright lights in the restaurant. Michael had sat next to her for the last two hours while they ate the traditional Christmas meal and enjoyed two bottles of Chardonnay. Staff from the offices and managerial teams were sitting around the long table enjoying their annual party night.

'The restaurant looks sensational with the gold and black Christmas décor and lights,' he said to Stella.

'Oh, yes,' she said. 'Along with the huge glittering tree in the corner of the room they've created a fabulous ambience.'

He nodded and sat back in his seat deciding she had different sides to her personality. In a usual male-dominated managers job, he found her intelligent, impressive, and strong. She was kind, caring and showed a vulnerable side in their friendship which he found charming. And in an intimate encounter like this, he thought staring into her eyes, she was attractive and oozed sensuality. Michael wanted to be with her.

The paper party hat from a Christmas cracker on the back of her head fell off and he put his hand on her neck to retrieve it. He felt her skin quiver under his touch which fuelled his feelings of desire.

'My hair's too thick, it keeps slipping off,' she giggled and wrinkled her nose.

He'd grown to like that wrinkle over the last few weeks and grinned at her. 'I love to see you laugh,' he said. 'It gives me a real boost.'

She twirled a finger through one of her curls. 'Same here,' she said. 'You've had such a miserable time lately.'

He nodded and sighed but shook the thoughts of Davina out of his mind.

She whispered. 'I love to laugh now-a-days. After all the horrid years I went through, all I want now is to have a little fun. I don't want anything heavy or troublesome with a man I just want to feel light-hearted and free.'

He sighed softly. 'Well, that is more than understandable.'

She hesitated and drew her fine curved eyebrows together. 'Dare I ask how things are with Davina?'

When she'd come across him in the canteen on the morning after Davina's birthday, Michael had told her everything about the last nine weeks. He'd ranted and raged about the insult and encouraged by Stella, he had blurted out the whole story. She had listened, understood his sense of injustice, and agreed with him about the unfairness of the comment. She'd patted the back of his hand sympathetically and made cooing noises in all the right places. Her advice had been to give Davina space, leave her to her own devices for a while, and stop running around after her.

He smiled now realising how good Stella's advice had been and although his marriage seemed to be at stale mate, he had his pride back firmly in place and felt better about the situation.

'Yeah, of course you can ask,' he mumbled leaning closer to her ear. 'Davina is working from home on a big project this week. All I can say is that nothing has changed. Its status quo, but I really don't want to talk about it tonight. In fact,' he breathed harder into her ear, 'I don't even want the thoughts of my marriage in my mind.'

He could smell Obsession perfume in her hair and on her neck. She felt warm and inviting. He lingered longer than he should have.

'There are a few people looking at us,' she whispered. 'I couldn't give a toss if they gossip about me and I do love having you close to me, but if you don't want to be the subject of office tittle-tattle on Monday morning, you'd better sit back a little!'

The quiet Christmas carols suddenly ended, and everyone turned in their seats to look behind at a DJ in the back of the room. He yelled, 'Merry Christmas, everyone,' and the words from Slade's Christmas song boomed through the sound system, 'Are you hanging up your stockings on the wall.'

There were cheers from their party around the table and everyone jumped up then hurried onto the dance floor.

'What do you think, fancy a bop?' he asked pushing his chair back. 'It's been a while since I danced but I'm willing to step on your toes anytime!'

She giggled and leapt up from her seat. 'I'd love to, Michael. Let's really get in the mood for Christmas.'

The red flowing material in the dress she wore had a deep V neck and a huge gold clasp. It looked as though the clasp was straining against her big chest to keep them in place. He tried hard not to stare.

When she bent forward to place her bag under the table the soft material gaped, and he caught sight of a red bra making the most of her voluptuousness. He licked his dry lips and moved his chair aside for to clamber across the seats. Finally, he took her tiny hand and propelled them both onto the dance floor.

The girls who worked in the finance department held their arms above their heads singing and swaying to the chorus, 'So, here it is Merry Christmas everybody's having fun.'

Michael jiggled himself and Stella next to them. With a flushed and happy face Stella cried out in glee as they bumped and grooved and laughed together through more dances.

She looked ecstatic and totally carefree, he thought, and was feeling the same himself. He was also drunker than he had been for a long time. After the second glass of wine when he usually stopped and moved onto soft drinks, he decided there was no point in holding back while he and Davina weren't even trying to conceive. So, now his head was reeling, his legs were making silly dance-like movements all on their own, and he felt happily intoxicated.

The small dance floor was packed with women glistening in their gold and silver party dresses. All the men had long since removed their jackets, and everyone seemed through his drunken blur, to be thoroughly enjoying themselves.

'Oh, I love this song,' Stella squealed excitedly and put her hands onto his shoulders. Unable to stop himself, he put his arms around her petite waist and pulled her towards him. He was sweating now with the heat of so many packed bodies together and he could see her top lip moisten while they swayed gently along to George Michael crooning, 'Last Christmas I gave you my heart.'

As hard as Michael tried, he couldn't hide his passionate feelings and felt his trousers tighten. When she snaked her arms around his neck and he felt her chest pushed firmly against his, he figured she felt the same. The soft mounds of flesh felt glorious against his ribs, and he nuzzled his nose into her hair.

Dreamily, she whispered. 'I've dreamt of having you close to me like this for weeks now but never believed I could be so lucky!'

He spread a hand down towards the small of her back and moaned softly. 'Oh, me, too.'

She said, 'You know, the first day I met you with Anthony, I thought you looked like Liam Neeson. And, for the record, I think Davina must be made of stone to ignore you. I know I wouldn't be able to keep my hands off you.'

At the mention of his wife's name, he shuddered with a small jolt. But then he reasoned, nobody could blame him if he did have an affair with this gorgeous woman. And, if Stella thought he looked like a film star, he thought giddily, who was he to argue. He was frustrated, lonely and unhappy at home with Davina. After all, he was only a man with normal needs. And one desirous need was now bulging.

When the song finished Stella asked, 'I'm sweltered, fancy some fresh air?'

He nodded and grinned while she took his hand, pulled him off the dance floor, and through a side door which opened onto the outside pavement in a back lane.

***

'Phew!' She panted and lifted the curls up from the back of her neck. 'It's far too hot in there!'

When she'd moved and positioned her arms up to her neck it had pushed her chest further together and upwards until Michael thought they were winking at him. Feeling very light-headed with a mix of alcohol and fresh air, he decided he couldn't fight it any longer. He plunged his face into her cleavage and inhaled her sweet soft smell.

Stella brought her arms down slowly and put both her hands onto his head pushing him further into her while she moaned his name repeatedly. He eased her gently against the wall and she threw her head back in ecstasy pleading for more.

'Oh, Stella, you're fabulous,' he mumbled.

With trembling fingers, he tried to undo the gold clasp but failed.

She began to giggle. 'Sorry, Michael, it doesn't open. It's just on the dress for decoration.'

He groaned in frustration and felt bereft. 'Never! What a tease,' he said, lifted his head up and chortled.

She joined him laughing and said, 'Look, why don't I go back inside, get my bag, and we could go back to mine for coffee? Then we can play together for hours?'

She had a drunken hapless smile on her face, and he agreed.

Waiting for her outside the main doors to the restaurant, Michael decided the fresh air had different effects on them. She was drunker, but he could feel himself sobering up rapidly. They climbed into the back of the taxi, and she placed her hand on his leg while he leant away from her and laid his hot forehead against the cold window.

Stella changed position and then laid her head against his cheat, and he knew he should wrap his arm around her. But in his befuddled state, he realised she wasn't Davina. She didn't feel or smell like his wife and he knew in that instant, neither the voluptuous Stella, nor any other woman, could ever take her place.

The recently applied spray of cloying perfume wafted up into his nose while she turned her face upwards to kiss him. Her chest was eye level to him and even though minutes before he'd had his head buried amongst it, now he felt as though he was suffocating. His heart began to thump, a pain developed in the side of his head, and the hurriedly eaten four course meal was threatening to make an escape. He gulped down a mouthful of vomit in his throat.

'Sorry, I'll have to get out,' he mumbled when the taxi driver pulled up swiftly to the Cedar tree in the village. 'I can walk from here.'

Apologising profusely, he climbed out of the taxi and vomited into the gutter. He looked up to see her disappointed face at the window when the taxi pulled away from the kerb.

Chapter Fourteen

Davina had heard Michael come home late from his Christmas party and when he'd rolled into his side of the bed, she had caught a faint smell of vomit on his breath. Surely not, she'd thought. Never, in all the years that she'd known him, had he drunk so much that he would throw up, not even in their early days when they'd loved the clubs and pubs in the city centre.

When he'd left to go to the Christmas party, she'd decided, if he came home in a good mood, she would snake her way across the space between them in bed. The gap seemed like a great abyss. She hoped that if she made love to Michael in their usual loving manner, it might help to rid her mind of the repulsive memories with Stewart.

Now, at nine in the morning he was still fast asleep. She'd been up from six, battling against morning sickness but had eaten two dry biscuits and the queasiness had gone.

In her pink pyjamas she perched on his side of the bed and stared down at him while he slept. Davina knew she'd hurt him deeply with what she classed as a silly throw-away remark on the night of her birthday. And she had also yelled at him which was something neither of them ever did.

She'd felt so guilty and ashamed that she hadn't really known what she was saying. Her whole mind and body had been in what people call, melt-down at the memory of her lewd behaviour. The fact that she'd even been capable of doing it had shocked her to the very core. She could of course have blamed the alcohol. But when she had dragged Stewart into that alley and kissed him, even though her head had been swimming, she'd still known exactly what she was doing.

Gently, she traced a finger down the side of Michael's arm and wondered how, if at all, she could put things right between them. He was the love of her life and still was one of the best men she knew.

Sensible, steady, and dependable might not be qualities some women looked for in a man but in a marriage, that she'd always thought would last forever, they were the building blocks she wouldn't want to live without.

He was loving and caring in his mild-mannered way and although quietly spoken, which others may think boring, he did have a dry sense of humour which still made her laugh. Lisa used to call him, the strong silent type, which she mused, was a good description. But when roused, he could also be dynamic especially when they were making love.

They'd both learnt over the years how to please each other's bodies and in her eyes, he had become a master in fore play rousing her quickly to a special place. The comment about him pawing at her was so unjustified and she didn't know why or what had made her even think of the words.

She sighed deeply knowing how much she'd hurt his feelings. When he found out about the baby and the fact that it wasn't his she couldn't imagine what it would do to him. She squeezed her eyes tight shut. More than anything else, he would be so disappointed in her. But there again, she shrugged, he couldn't hate her more than she already hated herself. Laying a hand over the small mound in her belly, she knew she could not delay much longer. She would have to tell him soon. What version of the truth she was going to tell him, she still hadn't decided? He stirred and stretched his long legs which she knew meant he was waking, and she scrambled up off the bed then headed downstairs to make coffee.

*

Michael opened his bleary eyes with a headache pulsating in his temples. The memories of the night before crashed back, and he groaned in misery hiding his head under the duvet. What in God's name had possessed him to behave like that? He remembered how he'd felt with Stella and how attracted he had been to her. She was an enticing woman, and he was frustrated. When he'd buried his face in her chest, he wondered now if it had been more of a longing for comfort than desire. And, of course he had drunk far more than he was used to lately.

He scolded himself and sighed, there was no point in making excuses. He'd nearly cheated on his wife and when he remembered vomiting in the gutter, he cringed. He had behaved like an irresponsible teenager. It had been the physical action of feeling sick that had stopped him going any further. He sighed with relief knowing he could have woken up in Stella's bed this morning and not here.

Swinging his legs over the bed he headed into the en suite and brushed his teeth vigorously trying to get rid of the stale taste of vomit. He used Davina's mouthwash and rinsed it around his mouth gargling the liquid in the back of his throat until his mouth was tingling with minty freshness.

He could text Stella and apologise for his ridiculous behaviour but decided to leave it until Monday morning when he would tell her in person how sorry he was. Hoping he would be able to get their working relationship back onto a friendly basis he picked up his shirt and trousers from the floor.

When he chucked the shirt into the laundry basket a whiff of her perfume filled his nose which made his stomach roll once more. He shook his head, deciding it had been a narrow escape then gingerly headed downstairs where he could smell fresh coffee from the percolator.

Later that morning when Davina agreed they should start Christmas shopping they left home to drive into Leicester. They wandered pleasantly through the shopping centre then stopped for a nice lunch. His hangover had shifted, and he felt much happier. More than he had for weeks.

'I don't suppose we can buy your mum perfume again this year?' Davina asked stopping at the counter in John Lewis where a young sales assistant was gift wrapping fragrance for a customer.

Michael stood next to her. 'Hmm, I suppose not,' he said smiling. 'What do you buy a woman who hardly ever leaves her home?'

His mum, Lorraine was like a recluse in their cottage. She rarely went out now-a-days and over the last few years, they'd worried that she was becoming depressed or agoraphobic.

Lorraine had worked all her life as a dinner lady in the local comprehensive school and had often said when she retired, she wanted to sit in a chair all day and do nothing. They'd scoffed and teased her, but sadly now they knew she had meant the declaration.

In summer she was to be found in her garden and greenhouse all day long and in the winter, she sat in front of the TV reading and knitting. Michael's father, Sam, reassured them frequently that she was happy and content. And he'd never heard her complain. She just didn't want to go anywhere.

Davina shook her head. 'It's unbelievable that she wants to live the rest of her life like this, but if she does, there's little we can do about it,' she said. 'We'll have to think of another gift.'

She moved further along to shelves displaying gift sets and picked up a gardening pack with gloves, small tools, and hand lotion. Davina showed it to him. 'This might work, and if we can't do anything to entice her out of the cottage, we'll just have to buy her things she uses every day.'

Michael grinned in agreement and then chose a gift set with aftershave and shaving foam for Sam.

They wandered over to the outdoor marketplace and stood stamping their feet together to keep warm. In front of the corn exchange, The Salvation Army band were playing a range of carols with a group of local schoolchildren, and he looked wistfully at the children's faces while they sang, 'Oh little town of Bethlehem.'

He could see Davina shiver in the chilly wind and instinctively put his arm around her shoulder. She leant towards him and snuggled into his shoulder. She looked beautiful this morning and when he thought of how close he'd come to cheating on her with another woman, he shuddered.

A little dark-haired boy stood in front of them with a collecting tin and looked up at her with huge brown eyes. Michael watched her face soften and smile at him bending down to drop two-pound coins into the tin. She would make a lovely mum, he thought, for the umpteenth time in the last few years.

He tried to understand how disillusioned she must feel at their failure. Maybe Anthony had been right, and she was just bone-weary of it all. Anthony had also told him that all marriages go through rough times and just because theirs had gone smoothly up until now it didn't mean it would always be problem free. Feeling more optimistic he took her hand and they ambled back to the car park and returned home.

Chapter Fifteen

The following morning, she told Michael that she intended to have a few more days off work to finish her project. And while at home she would do Christmas jobs from the list they used every year. Neither of them was the type to leave everything until the last week of December, and because they both worked full time it usually meant doing things on an evening.

They'd bought cards the day before at the charity shop and sitting at the dining table in front of her laptop she began to write them out with funny little messages inside for close friends.

She remembered yesterday's shopping trip and sighed. While they'd waited in a queue at the checkout with the giftsets, she'd stood close to Michael and inhaled his usual fresh Hugo Boss. His black polo neck jumper had heightened his clean attractive face and she had wished again that she could turn the clock back to their holiday.

She frowned staring at the cards. Davina knew she must have been temporarily insane to push this lovely man away. The thought of losing him when he found out the truth, brought a huge ball of misery into the back of her throat.

There were three cards to post overseas and just as she licked a stamp, she heard a knock at the door. Hurrying downstairs she found Emily, their next-door neighbour's, six-year-old girl.

'Mum says I can ask you to come to the n nativity play at school this afternoon,' she said.

Davina's heart melted. She obviously stumbled over the word nativity and was extraordinarily proud of the fact that she'd managed to say it. Her brown hair was tied up in bunches with pink ribbon and a big cheesy grin on her face.

Davina said, 'Thank you, I should be able to make it, Emily, what time does it start?'

Emily clutched a doll to her chest. 'My dolly is going to be baby Jesus and my name for today will be Mary.'

Emily's mum, Kate, put her head over the fence. 'Hi, Davina. It starts at two and when I noticed you were off work, Emily asked if you could come along.'

Davina smiled. 'Yeah, I'm working from home on a special project, but I'll try and squeeze it in,' she said then tickled Emily under the chin. Emily hopped excitedly from one foot to another in pink dungarees and ran back around the path giggling.

**

The local school hall was packed when Davina walked inside. Proud Mums and Dads had obviously got there early for front row seats to watch their little ones in the play. Kate waved to Davina, and she sat down next to her. An excited buzz ran through the room with subdued chatter. Kate told her how excited Emily was to be chosen for the leading role, and Davina looked at the children's artwork displayed on the walls.

There were Christmas nativity scenes, snowy North Pole scenes, and big fat Santa Claus pictures with each child's name and age at the bottom. Red, green, and gold paper chains were criss-crossed hanging from the ceiling with old-fashioned paper lanterns.

Davina thought the decorations looked a little jaded but the artificial tree in the corner of the room was spectacular. Bright colours of tinsel were draped around its branches, baubles of different shapes hung on clips, and three sets of white lights twinkled.

A thought floated into Davina's mind while she smiled at Kate. If she stayed in the village this would be where her child would come to school, and gingerly she stroked her bump under the thick wool coat.

The play began with teachers gathered around the little stage. Two of the children forgot or stumbled over their lines but were encouraged by parents with nods and smiles.

The drama teacher narrated the story of the birth of Jesus stopping every now and then for each child to say their lines. Emily emerged onto the stage grinning from ear to ear carrying her doll wrapped in a shawl followed by a boy called Joseph. She sat down and placed the doll into the crib while everyone in the room sang, 'Away in a manger no crib for a bed.'

While the teacher told the audience that Mary was carrying her baby, Jesus, the son of God, a small boy sitting next to her turned to his mum and asked if Jesus didn't know who his daddy was.

Davina smiled at the naivety and genuine simplicity of the question and then thought of her own baby who would be born not knowing who their father was. She could feel tears sting the back of her eyes but thought lovingly of her baby growing inside. He or she would be too little to understand or know about parents for months. It would only be the adults that were affected by the birth.

In a quiet but meaningful voice the drama teacher described how the great news spread and the shepherds and kings brought gifts because the birth had given so much joy to people.

Unable to stop the tears Davina let them flow down her cheeks. She'd been so traumatised about herself, Michael, and Stewart's feelings it suddenly dawned upon that they didn't really matter. It was her baby that was important. It was the love and happiness he or she would bring that would be magical.

She wiped the tears away with the back of her hand.

Kate gently touched her arm and asked, 'Are you okay?'

'Davina smiled back reassuringly. 'Oh, yes,' she muttered. 'It's just my blooming hormones!'

After mince pies and tea in the hall she walked briskly home in the frosty winter afternoon. A light flurry of snow had started to fall, and she felt a snowflake land on her lip. She licked it off with her tongue as she had done when she wasn't much older than Emily.

These were all the experiences her child would have, and she determined to be the best Mum possible, no matter if the father was present or not. If Michael left, and Stewart wasn't interested then she would bring up her baby alone. She wouldn't be the first woman to do this and as her mum would say, she certainly would not be the last.

She thought of her mum, Liz and wished she could tell her about the predicament. If there was ever a woman who could think through problems in a down to earth, logical way it was her. But she couldn't tell her, especially not about Leeds. Out of love for her only daughter, she knew her mum wouldn't say the words but disappointment and shame at Davina's behaviour would burn in her eyes. And she couldn't bear to see it.

They'd always been very close. Her father, Tommy, had worked offshore on oil rigs all his life therefore, Davina had spent weeks and months without seeing him. But even though her mum had worked as an auxiliary nurse in an old people's nursing home, she'd always managed to be there for her.

When she arrived home, she put a Christmas carol CD on the player downstairs and while the music wafted upstairs, she softly sang the words to each carol while soaking in a hot bath.

She closed her eyes and placed her hands over her bump gently talking to her baby. She was going to get to know her baby and love it so much before the birth that it might salve her conscience for the lack of interest so far. In the warm steam she felt herself drifting off to sleep imaging what her baby would look like.

At the touch of a cold hand on her shoulder she jerked awake and screamed. Her heart raced in fright until she realised it was Michael who was home early from work.

'Hey, it's only me,' Michael reassured. 'Sorry, I should have called out first.'

The level of bath water didn't quite cover her belly and she looked down following his gaze at the small mound. His mouth dropped open and his eyes bulged as if they were standing out on stalks, then slowly dragged his eyes up to meet hers.

When leaving the school earlier, she had decided to tell him when he got home from work. She had practised opening the conversation with, Michael, I've got something to tell you, or Michael, I'm pregnant, or Michael, you'd better sit down I have news.

Now, she figured that was unnecessary because he'd seen the baby for himself.

'D…Davina?' he stammered.

She began to sob and nodded her head. 'Yes, Michael, I'm pregnant.'

He licked his dry lips, and she could almost see his mind whirling in disbelief. He shook his head. 'I…I can't quite believe this is happening, are we going to have a baby?' He croaked. 'After all the years of dreaming about it, here you are lying in the bath with my baby inside you.'

She heard him catch a sob in his throat. He asked, 'C…can I touch it?'

She squeezed her eyes shut wanting to blot out the look of sheer amazement on his face. He looked like little Emily had at the play as though something so wonderful was happening he couldn't grasp the enormity.

She nodded her head slowly in consent. 'Yes, of course you can.'

He laid his hand gently over the mound and stroked it lightly with his long fingers. 'There's a part of me growing inside you and we'll be a family at last,' he said. 'I'll have my own son or daughter.'

She watched a solitary tear escape from the corner of his eye and run down into his beard. The feel of his hand on her skin in the soapy water was blissful. They hadn't touched each other for what seemed like an eternity, and she revelled in their loving connection.

How in God's name was she going to tell him it wasn't his? She just couldn't do it and panicked. There was no way she could bring so much devastation down upon him. But it's wrong, she raged staring up at the ceiling. She knew it was wrong on so many different levels, but she just couldn't shatter him with the truth.

'Why?' He muttered wiping his wet cheek. 'Why didn't you tell me?'

His words shook her back to reality. 'Look, let me get out, the water is cool now,' she said using the sides of the bath to lift herself up.

He grabbed a large towel from the radiator and wrapped it around her.

'I didn't realise until last month,' she explained. 'When I was sick at work, I thought I just had a tummy bug. And I was afraid I would jinx it if I told anyone. Which I know now is stupid but that's just the way I felt.'

He frowned. 'But I'm not just anybody, I'm your husband.'

'I know but I felt terrible because I was so horrible to you on my birthday,' she said and shivered. 'And since then, well, we haven't been very close.'

He nodded then sighed and rubbed her shoulders dry.
'Okay, so, I was giving you some space,' he said.
'Although now I feel guilty because you've been going
through all of this on your own.'

She snuggled into his chest. She bit her lip knowing her
next words should be, but the baby is not yours, at least I
don't think it is, but I won't know for definite until the
birth. She shook her head knowing she wouldn't get the
words out of her mouth and swallowed hard.

He shouted, 'But, I should have been there for you! It's no
wonder you didn't want to make love because your
hormones would have been all over the place,' he said.

She sighed. 'I'm sorry. I should have told you earlier, but
it's been a hell of a shock to me too.'

He wrapped his arms around her. 'Of course, it has, but I
wish you'd told me because I've been going nuts worrying
about you! It hadn't dawned upon me that you could be
pregnant because we've spent so many years dreaming and
wanting it to happen. I can't believe it's real.'

She saw the excitement and elation in his eyes now and he
picked her up in the air then swung her around. 'We're
having a baby!' He yelled delightedly at the top of his
voice.

'Michael put me down,' she pleaded feeling the mince pie
lurch dangerously up into the back of her throat. 'I might be
sick on your shoulder.'

'I don't care,' he shouted. 'Be sick anywhere you want to!'

But gently he placed her back down onto her feet. 'Sorry,
darling, I'm just so excited, all our dreams have finally
come true at long last,' he said. 'I'm going to look after you
and the baby properly, especially now that I'm going to be a
father.'

She saw the sheer delight shining out of every pore in his
body and guilty thoughts tried to push their way back into

her mind. But she thought of her baby, who was more important than anyone and determined to enjoy their happiness.

Chapter Sixteen

Although Davina had begged him not to tell anyone about the baby until they'd told both their parents on Christmas Day, he hadn't been able to contain himself and told Anthony.

Unexpectedly, he had grabbed him by the arms and hugged him. 'That is amazing news, Michael!' He'd shouted.

Stella had been an absolute star when he had apologised about the Christmas party and wished both, him, and Davina, all the luck in the world.

The Christmas products were launched successfully, and he'd ordered a large three-bird joint along with a piece of pork for Boxing Day. Most days in the run up to Christmas, he wandered around with a hapless grin on his face feeling so cheerful that he could burst. He told Davina they were going to have the best Christmas ever.

In the lounge, their usual red, gold, and green decorations were in place, and a fresh pine tree was dressed by them both with Davina placing the angel on the top.

'I was just thinking,' he said to Davina, 'I could pop into town and look for the purple trees they had last year, if you still want one?'

She refused then laughed and lovingly placed the nativity scene arrangement with candles on the window ledge. By the morning of Christmas Eve all the gifts were beautifully wrapped and laid under the tree. Personalised cards for their parents had been delivered, and just as she was hanging two red stockings over the fireplace, he hurried through the door laden with bags of food.

'Is there anything left in the shops?' she asked laughing.

He stood behind her fingering the stockings. 'Just think, Dee, this time next year there'll be another stocking to put up for our little girl or boy?'

With a smile on her face, he watched her head upstairs to get ready for the church service at St. James in the village.

When she came downstairs, he had the log burner roaring in the fireplace, mulled wine and mince pies were ready for carol singers that would invariably arrive, and to leave out for Santa Claus.

Michael grinned. 'Oh, I nearly forgot to tell you, but I bumped into Lisa earlier at the shops. I didn't realise you hadn't told her about the baby,' he said. 'I'd assumed because you were off sick the girls would know all about it?'

He saw her face flush and decided she looked almost embarrassed. 'No, I haven't told anyone, Michael. Not until we tell the parents tomorrow. Which is what we agreed upon,' she quipped.

'Er, I know,' he said, 'but I thought with Lisa being such a good friend you would have at least told her. Anyway, she knows now because I blurted it out, Sorry.'

He saw her sigh with irritation and wondered why this had upset her so much.

Chapter Seventeen

On Christmas morning Michael stared dreamily at Davina and their bump. They ate a leisurely breakfast of scrambled eggs and smoked salmon. He felt excited with the thoughts of the day ahead. Not just because it was Christmas Day, but because they would be telling their parents the good news about the baby.

The night before they had sung carols together in church and when they'd left to walk home, he mentioned how Christmas Eve had always felt special. The still night had been frosty, and they'd been able to smell the pine needles on the huge Christmas tree in the square. Every window in the village had been lit up with lights and decorations. An air of expectancy had hung around them as they had walked arm in arm huddled together against the cold.

Michael had opened a bottle of Chianti, of which she had one glass and he'd finished the rest. Slowly and carefully, they had made love and relished in the closeness of each other's bodies again. At one point she had seemed tearful and told him it was the sheer joy of having him back in her arms again. He'd apologised for the distance he had created, and afterwards they'd snuggled close to each other, then instantly fell asleep.

'We saw three ships come sailing in on Christmas Day in the morning.' played loudly from the CD while they opened their stockings which hung over the fireplace.

Davina, as usual had filled the bottom of his stocking with Pick-a-Mix sweeties, sherbet lemons, liquorice, strawberry creams, and chocolate éclairs. Amongst these treats was a pair of silly socks with drunken reindeers, two small samples of after shave, and a big round badge, proclaiming, Christmas Cook. Michael proudly pinned it to his red jumper.

When she opened her stocking, she found the usual mix of Brazil and walnuts, a small bag of Turkish delight, little pots of Dove hand and body cream, and a green silk scarf that she had admired. When she unwound the scarf to fold into a triangle shape, a little plastic packet fell out onto the settee. It held a multi-coloured babies dummy.

'Ah, Michael,' she cooed fingering the dummy.

'Well, we couldn't leave out little junior on Christmas Day,' he said wrapping his arms around her waist. 'And just think, this time next year he or she will be here and probably leading us a merry dance!'

She nodded and wound the scarf around her neck admiring it in the big silver mirror hanging above the fireplace.

He came up behind her and splayed his hands across her bump. 'I love you so much, Dee,' he said. 'You've made me the happiest man alive.'

'Well, it's nothing you don't deserve, darling,' she said.

They smiled together in the mirror at each other. 'I feel like I did on our first Christmas together,' she said. 'I love you now with such intensity that sometimes it makes me catch my breath.'

He nodded. 'Me, too,' he said. 'It just gets stronger and stronger.'

He left her and walked towards the kitchen. 'Okay, those sprouts won't peel themselves,' he said grinning. 'I'd better get cracking with lunch while you dress the table.'

Michael sauntered into the kitchen, took his Christmas Cook apron and tied it around the waistband of his grey trousers then began to peel and cut crosses into the bottom of the sprouts. Everyone had their own traditions at Christmas, and he loved to uphold theirs. With the delicious aroma from the joint roasting in the oven, he sighed in blissful happiness.

Who would have thought two months ago when he'd felt in such despair and thought his marriage was on the rocks, that it could have turned out like this? He ought to have known better, he cursed. He should have had more faith in his wife. And should have known something serious had occurred for Davina to behave the way she had.

He tutted and dropped the sprouts into a pan of water. Being huffy and distant for weeks hadn't helped, and he cringed. His mum always said he'd been huffy since he was a toddler especially when he didn't get his own way. He couldn't remember the childhood incidents she often quoted but his dad confirmed them, so, he figured they had to be true.

He peeled the skin from a parsnip and thought of his parents who were neither huffy nor sulky. Michael wondered, not for the first time, if it was because he had no siblings. Whatever it was, he figured, it was a weakness in his personality and something he needed to work on because he didn't want his child growing up with a huffy, grump of a dad.

He danced a little jig towards the fridge singing the words aloud from the next carol, 'Hark! The Herald angels sing Glory to the new-born King.'

Michael grinned; he was going to be a dad, and this time next year he would have a child to love and cherish. His family would be complete.

Davina had extended the dining table to its full length, and it looked sensational. He noticed that she'd bought new gold napkin rings, a gold runner to go down the centre, and large gold platters which would fit perfectly with their white dinner service. The candelabrum in the centre was gold with three white tapered candles but she hadn't lit them yet.

Their parents didn't usually arrive until twelve thirty for drinks and gifts. And, of course, this year would be slightly different because he intended to open a bottle of Champagne and announce the baby.

A sharp rap on the front door startled them both.

Michael frowned. 'Who can that be calling on a Christmas morning?'

'I'll get it,' she said and hurried down the stairs. 'It might be little Emily.'

Chapter Eighteen

While she descended the stairs, Davina grinned. She had Michael back and felt so much happier that she hardly recognised herself from the last few weeks. She still had the niggle of guilt in the back of her mind, but in church last night, she'd begged the lord for forgiveness. Surely, God would understand her need to protect Michael from devastation and upset?

Last night she had relished in the security of his strong arms and chest. He'd always made her feel she could climb mountains when he was beside her and she doubted now whether she would have had the confidence to stride ahead in her career without his unfailing support.

When she thought of work, she frowned knowing Lisa would be upset because she hadn't told her about the baby. She placed her hand over the baby and repeated the mantra, it doesn't matter, none of us are as important as you are.

Pulling the door open she expected to see their neighbours, but she froze in absolute horror. It was Stewart.

He stood with his arms folded across his chest. 'So, when, if ever,' he snarled. 'Were you going to tell me you are pregnant with my child?'

'Oh, My, God, she gasped.

Her heart hammered against her ribs so violently that she felt light-headed. She put a hand on the wall to steady herself while her mind raced. Her whole body began to tremble.

The noise of a pan lid falling to the floor in the kitchen reminded her of Michael and she knew she had to act quickly. She had to get Stewart away from the doorstep. Taking the arm of his thick leather jacket she pulled him inside the hall.

His face was red, and beads of perspiration stood along his rough forehead. He started to gabble, 'Lisa told me last night that you were pregnant. She was drunk and made a pass at me, but I knocked her back. S…she knew we had spent the night together in Leeds because she saw you creeping back to your room in the morning, and she screamed at me that I was wasting my time sniffing around you!'

Davina closed her eyes and cringed at the coarseness of Lisa's words. She took a deep breath and wiped her sweaty palms down the side of her green dress.

Struggling to think of what to say that might calm him down she opened her mouth but couldn't form any words. 'I…I.'

'Well,' he yelled. 'If what Lisa tells me is true and you've been trying to get pregnant for seven years with no luck then it's got to be mine, hasn't it?'

The actual words spoken in anger about her precious baby made her bristle. How dare he criticize their failure like this? She lifted her chin. 'I don't know,' she hissed standing with her back against the door. 'And the doctor tells me DNA testing isn't possible until after the baby is born. So, I won't know until next year!'

His fists clenched and there was a wildness in his eyes which scared her. She knew that shouting back at him wasn't going to calm the situation.

She changed the tone of her voice. 'Look,' she cajoled. 'I was going to tell you, but I've been really sick and I just c…can't seem to get my head around what's happened.'

'You can't?' he snorted. 'How the hell do you think I feel? I was told that I'm going to be a father by that twisted, jealous, Lisa, you call your friend!'

Davina couldn't believe Lisa had done this. Her mind spun with mixed up thoughts about their friendship. She remembered the click of a hotel bedroom door when she'd crept back to her own room that morning. But, even if Lisa had seen her, why had she told Stewart? After all the years they'd worked together she couldn't believe how jealous and embittered Lisa was towards her.

He folded his arms again across his chest and whereas before she'd thought the old leather was attractive now it made her shudder. His shoulders slumped slightly as though he was running out of steam.

This was her chance, she thought rapidly and begged, 'Please don't tell Michael, he doesn't know anything about us, and it'll kill him if he finds out today, of all days.'

He sneered at her. 'Well, I would think any day will be horrible when you find out your wife is pregnant with another man's child.'

She could feel the tears sting the back of her eyes at his cruel words. A wave of revulsion ran through her as she looked at his flabby face and thick neck. How had she thought him attractive in Leeds? She must have been temporarily off her head.

Davina tried again. 'Please don't tell him, Stewart. It's not going to make any difference to you whether he finds out today or tomorrow, but it'll make a hell of a difference to him.'

Michael appeared at the top of the stairs with a turkey baster in his hand. 'Davina,' he called. 'Who is it?'

She turned abruptly and looked up at her husband. 'It's Stewart from the ward,' she called back. 'There's been a big upset and he wanted to tell me about it.'

'Well bring him up for a drink?' Michael offered. 'Don't keep him standing down there, not on Christmas morning.'

Stewart followed her slowly up the staircase.

Her heart began to race again in trepidation. Stewart hadn't agreed not to tell Michael and she felt sweat run down her back. Would he tell him? From what she knew about his character on the ward, he was kind and considerate. But that was towards his patients and colleagues, which her and Michael weren't.

She'd managed over the last few weeks to keep the thought of DNA out of her mind but now it thundered back into her world. What would she do if it wasn't Michael's baby and Stewart claimed father's rights? She gulped and swallowed hard bracing herself for what was to come.

When Stewart reached Michael in the lounge, he shook his hand. 'I'm sorry, to bring bad tidings on Christmas Day, so to speak.'

Michael chortled at the pun and stood smiling at them wearing the apron which stated that he was a great Christmas Cook. She thought stupidly that he looked so principled and full of goodness that it brought a lump to her throat.

'Davina,' Michael said. 'Pour Stewart a whisky or something?'

On a small glass table in the corner of the room they'd set out bottles of rum, port, whisky, and sherry. She walked across and stood with her back to them and with trembling hands she poured large measures into two glasses.

She wanted to pour Stewart a small measure and get him out as quickly as possible but knew this would upset Michael's proprieties. She listened while Stewart told Michael that yesterday had been his last day on the ward and how he hadn't wanted to leave without saying goodbye. And, how they'd had an incident which he thought she should know about.

Davina walked back to both men and handed each of them a glass. She gripped the back of an armchair to still her trembling hands and looked beseeching at Stewart. Surely if he could see what a lovely guy Michael was he'd show them a little mercy.

Stewart had flung his jacket over the back of a dining chair, and she glared at it with resentment burning inside her. She didn't want him in her home especially not sitting next to her lovely husband. She bit her lip and silently began to pray.

'Yeah,' Stewart smiled mockingly. 'Someone has been stealing money from the nurse's lockers and I found I'd no other choice but to call in the police. The matron agreed but then I've begun to wonder if I'd done the right thing.'

Davina saw the look of outrage on Michael's face. 'Good God, who the hell would steal from nurses?' He exclaimed, 'They only get paid a pittance to start with!'

She let out the long breath she'd been holding and sighed softly in agreement.

'It's awful how sad things happen at Christmas time,' Michael said. 'When it should be peace and goodwill to all men.'

'I know,' Stewart said. 'But then afterwards I thought if there was a chance that the thief could be one of our own maybe I should have waited to see what Davina thought.'

Both men looked at her waiting for a response. She took a deep breath and rubbed her hands together. Stay focused, she thought, pretend you're at work dealing with a problem and everyone is looking to you for help.

'Well,' she croaked huskily. 'I think in this instance you did the right thing. The nurse who's had the money taken needs to know that every action is being taken to investigate the theft, even if it is someone on the ward.'

Michael nodded smiling. 'Yeah, and I think she's right.'

Stewart grinned. 'Oh, good. That's a comfort,' he said. 'Now I can head off knowing that Davina can pick up things when she goes back to work and that I've done the right thing.'

For one split second she wondered if there was a thief on the ward because he sounded so convincing. It was certainly a clever nonsense story that he'd made up as an excuse to call on Christmas morning.

While Michael took a swig of his whiskey, she raised an eyebrow at Stewart.

Stewart shrugged his shoulders. 'Well,' he said gulping the last of his drink. ''I'd better be going, and let you get back to your turkey.'

'Oh, it's not just a turkey this year,' Michael explained twirling the baster in his hand. 'It's what we call at work, a three-bird roast.'

'Wow,' Stewart said. 'That sounds amazing.'

Davina saw a look of genuine interest on Stewart's face while Michael told him how the three meats were rolled together and tied.

Stewart moved to the edge of the seat and Davina quickly grabbed his jacket from the chair. Her heart leapt in relief with the fact that he was leaving, and it seemed like he wasn't going to tell Michael the truth.

'Okay, then,' Stewart said standing up. 'And sorry again for bothering you on Christmas Day.'

Michael stood up at the same time and clapped him on the shoulder. 'Don't be daft, you did the right thing by coming,' he said. 'I love to meet Davina's friends no matter what day it is.'

Her smile was tight lipped while she handed Stewart his jacket. 'Yeah, thanks for calling but our parents will be here soon, and Michael has to get on cooking lunch.'

'Nonsense, there's plenty of time,' Michael cried. 'So, where are you going for Christmas lunch?'

Stewart moved towards the lounge door. 'Actually, nowhere this year. I'm leaving at four to drive down to London to my sisters. My parents are out in Spain and we're flying over tomorrow morning to join them, so we'll have our Christmas lunch tomorrow instead.'

'Not have Christmas lunch?' Michael gasped. 'That's a sin in my books, why not stay and join us for lunch, you can be our special guest.'

Noooo, Michael, she wanted to scream. Her knees weakened and she felt quite giddy. She grabbed the back of the leather armchair again for support. She couldn't bear the thought of having Stewart here another minute, let alone for hours over lunch.

'Oh, n…no,' she stuttered. 'I mean Stewart won't want to stay here for lunch.'

She moved behind Michael and wildly shook her head at Stewart begging him with her eyes to refuse the invitation.

Stewart smiled. 'No, I couldn't do that!' He said, 'It would be an imposition, and what about your parents? I mean, it's a family day.'

Davina rapidly locked into the excuse. 'Yes, Michael,' she said. 'What about your mum? You know she doesn't manage change very well.'

Michael turned and stared in puzzlement at Davina. 'Well, not in her own home but she'll be fine here. I'm sure they'll be delighted to meet one of your work friends.'

'Well, if, you're sure?' Stewart grinned. 'The roasted guinea fowl and duck combination does sound delicious!'

Davina knew she was sunk. Now that Stewart seemed excited about his roast, Michael would relish the chance to impress someone else.

At Michael's invitation, both men headed into the kitchen where she heard Stewart telling him that he'd spent several months working as a junior chef before his nursing career and how good food was one of his passions.

Davina slumped down onto the settee. She didn't know that about him, but there again she did not know much about him at all. Other than the fact he wore red and white boxer shorts and had a tattoo on his right arm.

She shuddered with the memories of that night but tried to rationalise her thoughts. If she was going to get through this ordeal, she must calm down and resemble a capable sane woman.

However, she decided, there was one positive outcome in the fact that the two of them were getting along well together. If Stewart really liked Michael, he might not tell him about Leeds. Also, if she could find it in herself to be friendly towards Stewart, and help to create a welcoming atmosphere, she just might get away without a horrible scene.

She took a deep breath when the front doorbell rang and knowing it would be Michael's parents, Sam, and Lorraine, she hurried downstairs.

Chapter Nineteen

'Hey, who does the bike belong to?' Sam asked after he'd kissed her cheek and wished her a happy Christmas. 'It's a real corker!'

She explained about her friend from work while they climbed the stairs. Amidst taking off winter coats, kissing their son and greeting Stewart, Davina didn't have time to fret. At the sound of more rapping on the door, Michael insisted on taking his turn down the stairs to welcome her parents, Liz, and Tommy.

'Oh, I'd love a sherry, Michael,' Liz said shrewdly looking Stewart up and down. Dressed in a classy white wool dress and black patent heels Liz smiled politely at the group. 'It wouldn't be Christmas Day without Harvey's Bristol Cream.'

Sam mentioned the bike to Tommy and the two men bombarded Stewart about how long he'd had it, what it drove like, then began to regale each other with memories of the bikes they'd ridden in the sixties.

After unwrapping their Christmas gifts and finishing their drinks, Michael called them all to the table. Davina had squeezed another place setting opposite herself for Stewart. He sat in between Michael's Mum and her dad. She knew Lorraine might struggle with conversation but was confident that her father, sitting smiling in his Christmas fair isle sweater, would have no problem keeping Stewart entertained.

Stewart turned to Tommy and commented upon how Davina looked like him. 'You mean she's got my big hooter?' he said laughing at his own joke.

At any other time, she would have felt irritated with her father for the embarrassment, but at this moment she couldn't have cared less. Liz came to her rescue and began to tell Stewart how she'd nursed old people for years but had to retire early at the age of fifty with a back disability.

Stewart nodded in understanding and a discussion took place about modern lifting techniques, hoists, and electronic lifts which Liz told them weren't around in the early days.

'So, Davina had plenty of encouragement to go into nursing?' Stewart asked politely fixing his gaze on Liz.

Liz smiled at Stewart warmly. 'Oh, yes. I've supported her all the way from the very start of her career.'

Michael insisted they all pull the gold Christmas crackers and wear their party hats to which Davina giggled nervously.

'You don't have to put it on,' she whispered across to Stewart when Michael had disappeared into the kitchen.

Usually, there was great merriment and excitement to see what tiny gifts were inside the crackers while they read aloud the silly jokes. But this year, she noticed, because of their guest, they were all being cagey and polite.

Stewart, however, made a great show of putting the red party hat on his head and pulling a ridiculous face at Lorraine.

Davina watched her mother-in-law, dressed in a plain blue pinafore which matched her mousey hair and the same large grey eyes as Michael. Lorraine fiddled anxiously with the paper napkin printed in a holly and ivy design.

Davina felt sorry for her. She was obviously out of her depth with this stranger sitting around their usual Christmas lunch table and she cursed herself for letting this happen. But she thought ruefully, she hadn't had any choice.

She glanced around the table avoiding Stewart's eyes. If either set of parents were perplexed at this surprise guest, they all had the good manners not to ask questions, but simply accepted his presence in good grace.

At Michael's request, Sam brought two bottles of wine to the table and walked round everyone offering red or white wine then filled their glasses. Davina thought she would be sick if she drank red wine and asked Sam for a small glass of white.

Her stomach rolled with nervous agitation, and she could see her mum looking at her with curiosity burning in her bright eyes. She would know there was something adrift; Davina thought sadly, because she had never been able to hide anything from her.

While they ate fresh prawn cocktails, Michael explained to Stewart how they were both only children and that his parents had lived in the next village all their lives. And, that Liz and Tommy had always lived in Leicester.

Stewart told them all about his childhood Christmas's spent in army barracks and the upheaval since his parents moved out to Spain in the summer.

Davina got up to clear the small plates away into the kitchen while Michael was busy loading tureens with steaming hot roast potatoes, sprouts, parsnip, and carrots.

'I thought we'd leave the announcement until after lunch,' he asked her eagerly. 'Is that okay?'

She looked at the happiness shining out of him and knew the reason he'd asked Stewart to stay was because he wanted to make a nice gesture to one of her work friends. She felt a twist of guilt in her already upset stomach. She knew now, that if she was lucky enough to get away without a hellish scene today, she would still have to tell him about Leeds. He deserved the truth, not lies.

While she helped carry the tureens of vegetables to the table, it suddenly dawned upon her that now Stewart knew about the baby, she would have no other choice but to include him in the upbringing of her child.

Michael's eyes were shining proudly when he carried the three-bird roast into the dining room and placed it onto the table. 'Do we have everything, Dee,' he asked.

The aroma of the cooked meat rose tantalising into the air, and she looked at the gravy jug, the cranberry sauce, and bread stuffing. 'Yes, Michael, I think we're fine,' she said smiling back at him.

'Great, now who wants what?' Michael asked ready to carve the roast. 'Or shall we all have a piece of each meat?'

Liz and Tommy agreed heartily telling Michael they loved all three meats, but Lorraine confessed she wasn't sure if she liked guinea fowl.

'Okay, Mum,' Michael reassured her. 'I'll cut you some plain turkey from the outer side of the roast.'

Lorraine smiled at her son as though he was a gift from heaven, and Davina realised this three-bird roast, as opposed to the usual large turkey, was indeed another change this year.

They all stared at the large joint while Michael began to carve through the succulent, tender meat varieties. Davina could see Michael's shoulders swell with pride when everyone congratulated him after tasting the different flavours from the duck, guinea fowl, and turkey.

Silence prevailed around the table while everyone tucked into the hot food, but she could only pick at her lunch. She had little appetite. Her favourite vegetable was sprouts but they had a weird taste, and she pushed them to the side of her plate. Whether it was because her mouth was dry with anxiety, or morning sickness, she wasn't sure but even the sweet parsnip felt like she was chewing gum.

She did manage two roast potatoes and three slices of carrot then saw her mum staring at her with a delicate eyebrow raised. Davina could tell she was mystified at her behaviour.

Stewart, she noticed, greedily wolfed down every mouthful of the meat and went into raptures about the flavour combination. Sam particularly enjoyed the fruity stuffing and Michael carved more slices for the four men.

Liz sat back and sighed contentedly. 'Michael that was absolutely delicious,' she said but refused a second helping. 'I'm leaving a tiny space for Christmas pudding.'

After the flaming Christmas pudding, Michael brought a bottle of champagne to the table. Davina followed behind him carrying a tray with seven tall, fluted glasses.

'Oh, my,' Lorraine quipped. 'I don't think I've room left for anything more?'

Michael walked around the table and stood behind Davina. He rested his hands upon her shoulders, and she took a deep breath.

Now that Michael was going to make the announcement, she prayed silently to herself that Stewart would have the good grace not to say anything. Surely, she thought, if he were going to tell Michael he would have done it by now? She hoped he would have the manners not to upset her family when they had all been so nice towards him.

She closed her eyes and began to count slowly to ten. It was a trick she'd learnt in sixth form, but she chastised herself, she wasn't waiting for exam results now. Mores the pity, she thought, at least she could manage her reaction to success and failure, but this situation was totally out of her control

Michael said, 'Well, although we didn't need to have an extra place setting at the table, we do happen to have two extra guests this year.'

Liz put a hand over her mouth then shrieked. Tommy cheered loudly. But Sam and Lorraine both looked at Michael in confusion.

Michael leant forward over her shoulders and gently laid a hand over Davina's flowing green dress. He stretched the soft material with his hands which revealed the small bump. 'I mean, we're going to have a baby!'

Her heart began to race. She didn't dare look at Stewart's face.

Liz jumped up from the table and clapped her hands in glee. 'Oh my, darling girl,' she exclaimed then reached across the table and placed both her hands onto Davina's cheeks. 'How far along are you?'

'I'm three months, Mum,' she said.

She tried hard to look and remain calm but jammed her quivering knees together under the table.

Sam took the bottle of champagne from Michael. 'Here, son, let me do that, I want to toast my first grandchild,' he said and popped the cork.

Lorraine and Liz both whooped with happiness and began to discuss knitting patterns and all manner of baby things.

Michael sat back in his chair accepting their congratulations and best wishes then beamed at everyone while they sipped the champagne.

Suddenly, Stewart scrapped his chair back away from the table. 'Excuse me everyone,' he said briskly. 'But I'll have to leave now to get on the road down to London.'

Davina jumped up with him. 'I'll get your jacket and show you to the door,' she said while Michael hurried around the table and pumped his hand.

Stewart thanked him for lunch and hospitality politely, nodded to the parents and strode quickly down the stairs with Davina quietly following behind him.

While he opened the front door, he leant forward staring into her face. 'He's a great guy and you have to tell him the truth. It's totally unfair not to,' he growled between his teeth.

She nodded numbly hardly daring to think that she'd got away without a scene. 'Thank you for not spoiling today by telling him. You can see what it means to him and if you had told him, he'd hate every single Christmas Day for the rest of his life.'

He pushed his arm through the sleeve of his jacket. 'I can see that, but on the day the baby is born, I want a DNA test done,' he said coldly. 'And, if it is my child, I'd like to have the same happy occasion that you've just had with champagne and my parents in Spain.'

She gasped at the thought of him taking her baby abroad. It filled her with terror, but she stifled the fear down with longing to get him away from the house.

'I'm going to text you in the New Year, Davina. And if you haven't told Michael by then, I will,' he snapped and narrowed his eyes. 'He has to be told and if you won't then I will, get it?'

She nodded and he walked away from the door then climbed onto his bike.

Chapter Twenty

At the roar of the motorbike pulling away from the drive she slumped back against the closed door. Her body felt weak and exhausted while the huge sense of relief flooded through her. She looked upwards to the top of the stairs hoping she had the strength to climb them.

If only Stewart had been the type of guy that would run a mile at the thought of family commitment, then she could have got away without hurting Michael. But Davina knew she had to do the right thing and tell Michael the truth. Apart from the fact that he deserved to know, she also knew that if she didn't, Stewart would. And, even though he was moving to Bournemouth, Stewart intended to exert his rights as the father.

When she reached the lounge, she apologised to everyone. 'I think I've eaten too much. I'm just going to take an hour's rest on the bed,' she said. 'I'm shattered.'

Michael instantly put his arm along her shoulder and walked her up to the bedroom. She lay down on the bed and he pulled the bedspread over her.

***

She really did look tired, Michael thought, and felt guilty that he'd been absorbed with cooking lunch and hadn't given much thought to her well-being.

'I'm fine,' she said when he fussed over her. 'Go back downstairs for The Queen's speech, you can't leave them alone sitting in the lounge.'

She was right, he knew, but he felt responsible for them both. He stroked the fringe away from her forehead. 'Okay, but if you don't feel well, you must tell me, and I'll call a doctor. Maybe the excitement of Stewart staying has been too much for you,' he said. 'What a nice bloke he is?'

He saw her eyelids droop as she murmured in agreement then closed her eyes.

After they'd listened to the Queen and her Christmas greeting, the five of them had stood and toasted her majesty which was a yearly ritual, then finished the champagne.

Lorraine and Liz began to talk excitedly about shopping sprees they could organise to baby shops in the city. A Christmas film with snowy scenes and penguins began and he told Sam and Tommy that this time next year they'd be watching the film with their baby grandson or granddaughter. With glasses of port the two older men dozed in their chairs while he sat next to his mum and allowed her to hug him tight.

He said, 'I hope you will be up for a spot of babysitting, Mum?'

She smoothed the side of his hair. 'Oh, yes. Of course, Michael,' she sighed longingly, and her eyes filled with joyous tears.

All his life, he'd tolerated his mum's clingy affections. Even now as a grown man when he looked into her eyes, he knew exactly how she felt about him, because it was the way he already felt about his baby. Although he'd appreciated his family and knew how lucky he was to have such doting parents, at the thought of being a father himself, the meaning of the word family had never been so significant.

Liz was full of questions about how long they'd known. How long Davina had been feeling tired. And if she'd had morning sickness. Michael could sense a touch of resentment in her tone that her daughter hadn't told her earlier, but he hoped by explaining how he'd not found out until late, it would help.

'And you don't find that a little strange?' Liz probed.

Although he had to agree with her, Michael stiffened his shoulders in Davina's defence. 'Well, because her monthlies were all over the place and because we've waited for years it hadn't dawned upon her that she could be pregnant. She thought the sickness was a bug she'd picked up at work.'

Liz nodded understandingly and Lorraine wrung her small hands together. 'But everything with the baby is okay, isn't it?'

He reassured and told them about the antenatal and produced a scan photograph. 'We decided not to know the sex of the baby until the birth,' he said. 'Davina reckons because the baby was a total surprise knowing if it's a boy or girl should be too.'

'Oh, how lovely,' Lorraine sighed.

Michael smiled at her. 'And that's not the only surprise I have for her,' he said. 'You know that we usually have a mini city-break during my week's holiday from work but this year I've booked us into a luxurious Spa hotel for some serious pampering. It has five stars, with gorgeous food, and a massive four poster bed, a swimming pool, sauna, and Jacuzzi.'

Both women sighed enviously.

Chapter Twenty-One

On Boxing Day, after Michael had returned from the football match and they'd eaten their way through a whole box of chocolates watching the film, 'It's a Wonderful Life.' Davina was ready to confess all.

Michael hadn't mentioned going away this year, but she knew he would be off work until after New Year. Once all the turkey's roasts had left the factory for the supermarkets it was quiet, and most staff took holiday.

She didn't want to leave it until the week after because Stewart might keep his word and tell him after New Year. She couldn't bear the thought of the horrible news churning around in Michael's head at work. If, what she thought would happen and he left her, it would be best to do it when he was on holiday.

That morning, she'd woken with a heart full of trepidation and sorrow. Those were the exact words, she had decided, brushing her teeth. Sorrow and sadness, that because of one night's reckless stupidity, she was going to lose the love of her life.

Davina made a pot of coffee and sat in the armchair looking at him chewing a chocolate toffee. Her mind tumbled trying to think of how to put the words into sentences that could explain her actions but decided there was no way she could soften the blow.

It was the same as telling people their loved ones had died on the ward, she thought. You simply had to say the words slowly and accurately, all the while knowing you were shattering their life as they knew it, into little pieces.

Michael finished sipping his coffee then looked at her and raised an eyebrow. 'What's wrong, darling,' he said.

Davina could tell he sensed she was in turmoil. They knew each other so well.

'I've got to tell you something horrible and I'm trying to find the words.'

She placed her coffee mug gently onto the coffee table and began. She took a deep breath and started with the way she had felt when they were in Turkey on holiday and how she'd longed for change and excitement.

Then she told him about Stewart and the attraction she had felt between them and how she'd got very drunk in Leeds. She stared down at the table and fiddled with a napkin tracing the pattern of the holly with her finger. The words choked in the back of her throat. She knew she had to get the worst bit over, but she couldn't bear to look at him when she told him what they'd done in the hotel.

*

'What!' he bellowed jumping up from the table. 'The guy that was here for Christmas lunch? You've been having an affair with him!'

The blood was pumping around his body at a rate of knots, and he could feel a vein in the side of his temple begin to throb. He shook his head in disbelief as though he hadn't heard her correctly. He felt like he was in the middle of a grotesque nightmare that he would soon wake up from. He couldn't grasp or take in what she'd just told him but when he saw the tears streaming down her face, he knew she was telling him the truth. She had been with another man. He hardly recognised his own voice because it sounded like a growl, 'How the hell could you make love to another man?'

*

His face was red and sweating, his nostrils flared, and his eyes were cold and hard. She wasn't scared because she knew no matter how mad he was he wouldn't hurt her. She whimpered, 'I...I don't know. But it wasn't making love, it was just sex.'

'Christ, it doesn't matter what words you want to use, you've been with someone else,' he snarled sarcastically. 'So, let's just get this right, you didn't want to have sex with me for weeks, but you did with him?'

She nodded miserably feeling her nose run and mix in with the tears on her face. 'It wasn't like that I was drunk,' she gabbled and swiped the napkin under her nose. 'A…and for once, I didn't have to do it to make a baby. For those two hours I just felt like a normal attractive woman again.'

'Two hours!' He shouted. 'Jeez, what is he, Goliath?'

Her mind was racing and muddled with the upset. She realised the mistake she'd made and stumbled, 'Nooo, we did it twice in two hours,' she tried to explain but when he picked up a tin of Quality Street chocolates and threw it at the wall, she knew she was making it worse.

*

He squeezed his hands tightly into fists trying to stay in control because he wanted to punch something. The thoughts of another man arousing her incensed him even further. His chest was tight, and he thought his head was going to explode as he began to pace around the room. He kicked the side of the settee. How could she? How could she go with another man? He shook his head and glared at her.

*

She was worried he was going to have a seizure or heart attack and knew she would have to try and calm him down 'I had to tell you, Michael,' she said quietly. 'And I know it's horrible but please take some deep breaths.'

He did as she bid and slumped down onto the settee breathing deeply in and out. Davina watched his breathing slow, and his chest begin to relax. She could tell he felt calmer and got up from the chair then made to move towards him. She saw the look of desolation begin to fill his eyes and knew it was dawning upon him that he might not be the father.

*

Michael put his hand out in front of her. At this moment he didn't want her anywhere near him. His mind was a whirl of mixed emotions and crazy thoughts. The long white T-shirt she wore over thick leggings made the bump look prominent and he suddenly remembered the baby.

The revolting idea that it wasn't his baby crashed into his mind. His mouth felt dry, and a mouthful of chocolate regurgitated into the back of his throat. Grinding his teeth, he had to ask the question. 'So, it's not my baby, then?'

She stood in front of him and placed a hand over her bump. 'I don't know,' she said and began to sob. 'W…we made love in Turkey and then Leeds was the following weekend. And the doctor explained that I cannot have DNA testing done until after the birth.'

Unbelievable, he thought sadly, after spending weeks thinking he was going to be a father, now it might not even be his. And then, it slowly started to register that considering they'd not been able to conceive in seven years it was a knocking bet it had to be Stewart's child.

Until now he'd only been able to think about her and how she had betrayed him but now an image from Christmas Day of Stewart, the smirking hulk, came to his mind. Right at this moment he hated her. 'And I invited that creep into my home for Christmas lunch when you've been seeing him at work?'

He saw her bristle and lift her wobbly chin. 'Look, I know I have to take the blame for all the mess I've made, but not yesterday's fiasco, that was out of my control,' she said. 'It was only that one night and I've never looked at him since. I…I hate him now.'

He thought of Stewart sitting around the table with his gentle mum and dad and he felt physically sick. 'And you let him sit here with our lovely, decent parents,' he shouted. 'Shame on you, Davina!'

'Oh, that's not fair!' She yelled back. 'I haven't seen him since the last day I was at work, but Lisa told him on Christmas Eve that I was pregnant then he turned up here yesterday demanding to know if he was the father. I tried my hardest to get him to leave but you insisted he stay for lunch!'

He was outraged with her pathetic reasoning. 'Christ! So, this is all my fault now, is it?'

Tears cursed down her cheeks again and he saw her swallow hard. 'No, of course it's not,' she said. 'But I was in the process of begging him not to tell you and spoil your Christmas Day when you invited him upstairs.'

'You little idiot,' he said. Contempt at the knowledge that they'd huddled together in the hall pitying him made him start to sweat. 'Don't you know the memory of him sitting at our Christmas lunch and eating my turkey will never leave me? And the humiliation of that is much worse than if you'd told me yourself!'

She sobbed. 'I know I should have told you the truth the day you found me in the bath, but how was I to know it would escalate into this,' she said quietly. 'It's because I love you so much that I didn't want your Christmas Day ruined. I honestly never thought for one moment that Stewart would just turn up here!'

Michael slumped back onto the settee and looked up at her. Her fringe was stuck to her wet tear-stained face, her blue eyes were red with crying, and her arms hung by her sides. His gorgeous wife, who he always thought he'd never tire of looking at, looked wrecked.

'Hmph,' he scathed. 'I'd much rather you'd told me the truth then I could have at least blacked his eye. And that way I would feel better. In fact, if he hadn't gone off to Spain, I'd find this Stewart Dunn and give him the pasting he deserves for screwing my wife and lauding it over me!'

Suddenly he felt the air was choking him and he had to get out of the room and away from her. 'I c...can't stay here with you,' he stuttered and ran upstairs into the bedroom. He pulled a holdall down from the top of the wardrobe and began to throw clothes into it then grabbed toiletries from the bathroom cabinet. She was waiting in the hall as he ran back downstairs and grabbed his car keys.

'Where will you go?' she begged and stared after him as he ran out of the front door.

Chapter Twenty-Two

Michael drove out of the estate and headed towards the canal where he pulled up in a quiet spot. He put his forehead on the steering wheel and choked back tears. He couldn't believe what had just happened in the last hour of his life. How could they go from watching a Christmas film and eating chocolates to this?

There were so many thoughts and feelings raging through his body and mind that he felt exhausted. Where and who to go to, he thought miserably. If he went to his parents, he'd have to talk about it, and if he landed on Anthony's doorstep it would be the same. He knew he couldn't talk to anyone, not while he was in a state of shock about what she'd done.

The brochure for Ragdale Hall was lying on the back seat of the car and he wondered if he should go alone? He'd booked a lavish expensive suite for them and knew it was probably a waste of money but remembered her betrayal when she'd been with Stewart in Leeds.

Why not, he thought, rang the hotel, and brought the date forward to that evening. He swung the car around and headed off to Melton Mowbray.

The impressive hall stood in acres of beautiful countryside. When he pulled up outside the front hall and clock tower, he whistled in awe. At only three levels high the stone building, with ivy growing around the large front sash windows, looked amazing. Just the place to unwind and sort his head out, he thought, carrying his bag into the reception.

The lady in reception greeted him warmly and showed him around the retreat, the beauty express, veranda terrace bar and pavilion seating area. He explained that Mrs Philips would be joining him later to which she smiled and gave him a key. When he opened the door to the luxury suite and saw the lovely lounge area decorated in grey and lime green, he sighed heavily. Davina would have loved this.

He wandered into the bedroom and flopped down on the huge bed squeezing his eyes tight shut. He hoped that if he kept his eyes closed, it might stop him thinking about her rolling around a hotel bed with the big oaf. However, it didn't stop the image flooding behind his eyelids.

Michael tried to think of excuses for her that would explain this behaviour which was certainly out of character. Perhaps he had drugged her? Or had he forced himself upon her? However, he knew that respectable men didn't want to be with a woman who was incoherent with alcohol.

He sighed. On Christmas Day, he'd got the impression that Stewart was a decent sort of a chap and a conscientious nurse. So, this didn't match either of his theories. Also, he thought, they'd done it twice in two hours, so she must have known what she was doing.

Tears pricked at the back of his eyes, and he sat upright. He needed a drink and went back into the lounge where a bottle of champagne was chilling in the ice bucket.

He popped the cork remembering the way his dad had opened the champagne on Christmas Day with such pride and happiness with their first grandchild. Tears choked him now as he gulped at the champagne hoping for numbness but decided it wasn't strong enough. He spotted a mini bar in the corner of the room and opened two small bottles of whisky tipping them into a large glass. After a large gulp he felt the whisky curse through his veins and went back into the bedroom with the bottles.

Michael lay on the bed drinking the whisky and replayed the whole argument in his mind remembering everything she'd told him. He wasn't going to be a father; he cried and couldn't stop the tears flowing down his face.

He took a deep breath and dried the tears away with the sleeve of his jumper. He tried to remember the last time he had wept. It was probably when he'd been a little boy and his biggest worry had been if he'd be chosen for the school rugby team.

It was too warm in the bedroom, and he stripped off his trousers and jumper and lay in his boxer shorts gulping at the whisky until his head swam.

The fact that she was pregnant with Stewart's child had hit him like a shot in the forehead. In the seven years that she hadn't been able to conceive, and although the words were never spoken between them, they had always assumed it was because of her reproductive organs. He cringed; it had never once been suggested that the problem lay with him.

But now he had to accept the fact that if she was pregnant with another man's sperm, the fault had to be with his equipment. He pulled his boxer shorts down and looked at himself. He frowned, but he'd had the tests done and the doctors said his sperm count was fine. The confusion spun around in his befuddled mind until thankfully he felt himself drifting off into a drunken sleep.

He woke in the early evening with a thick head and a dry mouth. Within minutes of being awake he remembered what had happened and padded into the bathroom where he swallowed bile down and tried not to vomit. He needed food and rang room service.

After eating, he instantly felt better and began flicking through channels until he found a football match to watch. Lying on the settee, he came to a decision. Because there was no action for him to take now when he didn't know how to manage the situation, he would stay at the hotel for a few days and revel in the luxury.

A text appeared on his mobile from Davina. She asked him briefly just to let her know that he was okay, and he quickly typed back, two words, 'I'm fine.'

He didn't want Davina to know where he was but also knew if he was in her position, he'd want to know at least that she was still alive and hadn't done anything damaging.

The next morning, he bought sportswear and swimming trunks then spent the day using facilities to deal with the upset in his mind. He trained in the gym, ran through the countryside for miles, and swam until his legs ached trying to quell the rage and temper he felt when he thought of her betrayal.

Later that night, after he'd drank a bottle of wine, and lay in the Jacuzzi bath soothing his aching calf muscles a text tinkled into his mobile. He hoped it wasn't from Davina because he wouldn't know what, if anything, he could say. He looked down onto the screen and saw the name, Stella.

It was a friendly text in which she hoped he'd had a great Christmas and wondered if he had plans for the New Year. He scrambled upright, grabbed a towel to dry his wet hands and wondered drunkenly if he should ring her? She would listen to him and offer advice as she'd done before. Or, he thought, draining the glass of wine, he could ask her to join him?

She was always looking for a little fun. Stella had told him this before and the Jacuzzi certainly was fun. He splashed at the bubbles and felt his spirit's lift. He remembered the Christmas party night and felt himself fill with desire at how glorious her chest was when he'd snuggled his face into her.

She was a gorgeous, attractive woman and he could have spent the night with her, but his conscience hadn't allowed him to do that. All because, he thought scathingly, she hadn't been his precious Davina.

Now, he snorted in disgust, when he knew what Davina had done in Leeds and thought of her writhing on a bed with Stewart, he wished he'd gone with Stella.

He climbed out of the bath, tied a towel around his waist and punched her number into his mobile. However, he remembered how he'd vomited in the gutter because her chest and cloying perfume had made him feel sick. And crying on Stella's shoulder wouldn't be fair to her. She was a nice lady and deserved more from him even as a friend. Slowly but deliberately, he switched the mobile off, threw himself on the bed in disgust and cried himself to sleep.

During the following day, the hotel staff were getting ready for the pending, New Year's Eve celebrations. Around six o'clock and after another gruelling exercise regime, he was swimming in the darkened indoor pool. He paused under the large fountain to let cold water pour down over his head.

A young couple in their twenties huddled together in the back of the pool near the thermal spa. She was giggling and he could hear the deep tones from the guy whispering things to her. She clung to him with her arms around his neck and Michael felt such a stabbing pang of loneliness and longing for Davina that it nearly took his breath away.

He sighed, but how could he long for her when she'd been with someone else? He tried to rationalise his thoughts knowing forgiveness wasn't one of his strong points. He swam to the edge of the pool, hauled himself out, and lay down on a sunbed.

It was the first time in his life that he'd ever been completely on his own and although he knew the time spent thinking had been beneficial, he didn't want to stay any longer. He wondered whether Davina had told their parents that he'd walked out. She could have rung Liz when he had left, and might be in Leicester with them? He couldn't face going back to his claustrophobic hotel room and wandered onto the veranda terrace bar.

He sat on a stool at the bar and ordered a gin and tonic. The girl behind the bar had the same hairstyle as Davina and he sighed heavily thinking of his wife. He'd always loved everything about her. The small chest, her long slim legs, her rosebud lips, and even her long nose. In fact, although she'd hurt him dreadfully, he still couldn't stop thinking about her and missed her presence.

They had never spent more than two nights apart in all the years they'd been married. And he felt like this rift was like a living hell. But if he went back to her he would have to bring up another man's child, and he wasn't sure he was capable of that.

'Penny for them?' A voice from a man sitting on the next stool startled him back to reality. He was a big burly guy in his late forties wearing a black business suit and rimmed gold glasses. A briefcase lay at his feet.

Michael huffed. 'You wouldn't want to know!'

The man lifted his glass and took a swig of his whisky. 'Try me, it'll take my mind off my problems for a while,' he said. 'My usual hotel is fully booked. So, I've had to pay double for this place or sleep in the car. And by the time I've paid for this work trip on expenses I'll hardly have made a fiver.'

Michael nodded wishing money were his only problem. But, he decided, it couldn't hurt to talk things through and starting at the beginning he told him everything.

'Hmm,' the man murmured. 'And do you think she loves him?'

Michael shuffled awkwardly on the stool remembering what Davina had told him. 'She reckons she hates him now and that she must have been temporarily insane to go with him.'

They ordered another drink and Michael relaxed into his company. He put his hand out to shake and the man introduced himself as John Staples.

John nodded and told him how his wife had gone to America with her new lover and had taken his two girls with her. They were divorced now, and he only got to see his daughters twice a year.

'Oh, that's terrible,' Michael said. He could see the pain in his big oval eyes. 'And do you still care about her?'

He shrugged his big shoulders. 'Oh, I've joined a dating site and met a few nice women, but no one comes close to her,' he said pensively. 'You see, no matter what she's done, I've never stopped loving her. She was the bee's knees.'

Michael nodded. 'Ah, I've been sitting here thinking how much I miss Davina and that I shouldn't even be thinking about her after what she's done,' he said. 'I guess I'm not that big on forgiveness?'

'Well, mate, we all make mistakes, and your wife certainly made a corker,' he said looking into his glass and swirling the whisky around. 'But if it was me, and if you think she still loves you, I would fight for her, and not let her get away. I know if I had another chance that's what I'd be doing.'

Michael rubbed the back of his neck wondering if he would be able to forgive her. He wasn't sure if he had it in him. And of course, there was still the baby to think about 'So, even if I could get my head around that, there's still Stewart's child to consider.'

'Now, you don't know that for sure, it could be yours?' John reasoned. 'Did you ever talk about adoption when you were trying for all those years?'

Michael thought back over the visits to the clinic and nodded. 'Yeah, they told us about the option at the fertility clinic and we both agreed that it would be a last resort, but we wouldn't dismiss the idea.'

'Well, try to look at it this way,' John said taking his glasses off and wiping them on a napkin. 'If this hadn't happened and in a few years' time you and Davina might have been in the process of adopting a baby?'

Michael shook his head. He couldn't follow what he meant and tugged on his ear. 'Er, you've lost me with that one.'

John smiled. 'I mean, what's the difference? If you had decided to adopt, you'd be bringing up someone else's kiddie anyway. And at least this way half of the baby is still hers, so it'll be part of your family, right?'

My family, Michael thought with a jolt. With a flutter of hope snaking around his stomach he wondered if they could make it work. Now he knew that at least he wanted to try. And if any woman was worth fighting for, it was Davina.

He clapped John on the shoulder and jumped down from the stool.

'Thanks, John,' he gabbled. 'And good luck with things.'

He ran up the stairs to his room taking them two at a time and threw his things into the holdall. They had a lot of talking to do and months of trying to make it work but the option of living without her would be worse. So much worse than what they had now.

Chapter Twenty-Three

After watching Michael pull away in his car Davina felt totally and utterly bereft. The shock and enormity of what she had told him registered in her mind. Although she'd known he was going to be upset and hurt, she hadn't expected the ferocity of his anger and temper.

She'd never seen him in such a rage before, pacing around the room and kicking at the settee. It was as though he had wanted to lash out at her. And who could blame him, she thought sadly. Obviously, he hated her now and the look in his eye when he'd snarled at her bump made her shiver.

Davina folded her arms across her chest and rubbed her hands up and down her arms in a comforting manner as if someone were cuddling her. She yearned for him and wished it hadn't happened so he would be as much in love with her as he'd always been.

Replaying the argument over and over in her mind she wondered if she could have said things in a different way or missed bits out. But she had got upset and told him more than was necessary which made it even worse. When she remembered telling him she'd done it twice in two hours with Stewart, she cringed and wailed aloud at her stupidity.

With a large mug of tea and two biscuits she spent the rest of the day wallowing on the settee worrying about Michael. She remembered the tortured look on his face, and knew as long as she lived, she would never forgive herself for hurting him so much.

Later in the evening she began to wonder where he'd gone and if he was with his parents. However, when the telephone rang, and Sam left a message for Michael, this told her he wasn't with them.

Well, my little Christmas miracle, she whispered soothing her bump, it looks like it's just you and I now, then wearily climbed the stairs to bed.

When Davian woke it was the first time she'd got up from the bed with no queasiness or sickness. She was ravenous. After a huge plate of bacon and eggs she pottered around the house tidying up after the Christmas festivities then went for a long drive.

The roads were quiet during the Christmas holiday and a strong winter sun beat down on the windscreen while she headed out of the village. Her mind was still full of Michael, but she concluded that there wasn't anything more she could do to put right what had happened. And she had lost him.

With her mobile on hands free in the car, a call from Lisa appeared on the screen and instantly she decided not to answer. Davina still couldn't believe what Lisa had done and said about her to Stewart. Although Lisa had been very drunk on Christmas Eve, the jealousy and bitterness shown towards her was too hurtful to cope with. An old saying came into her mind as she sat at traffic lights, hell hath no fury like a woman scorned.

***

When she returned home a note had been pushed through the door and her heart skipped a beat praying it would be from Michael. But when she retrieved it from the letter box, she cursed herself knowing if he had come back, he would have used his key.

The note was from her mum and when she walked into the lounge the answer machine was bleeping with a message. Mum wanted to go shopping to the sales. The thought of crowded shops depressed her, and she knew within an hour spent with her mum she would wheedle it out of her. She couldn't talk about Michael and what she'd done.

With a growling stomach, she wandered into the kitchen and opened the fridge. The remains of the three-bird roast wrapped in foil looked appetising and she cut off chunks then packed the turkey into a sandwich with fruity stuffing.

Smiling to herself she sat in front of the TV and couldn't believe that her pregnancy craving, out of all the lovely food in the fridge, was for turkey.

Twice since he'd left, she brought up his number on her mobile to ring him but didn't know what to say. There was nothing more she could say that would make the situation any different.

When darkness fell the house was deathly quiet and all she could hear was the pitter-patter of rain on the window. She turned off the TV and wandered aimlessly around the lounge. She missed him so much and knew in a way the heartbreak hadn't even started yet. The empty years ahead without him seemed very bleak and scary.

She stood in front of the Christmas tree remembering each bauble they had bought in all the various places they'd visited. A rock-star Santa Claus from the Xmas shop in York, and a blue and white snow scene was from Brighton Pavilion. She fingered a glass bauble with hand-painted mistletoe that she'd bought in Dorset last year and let the tears stream down her face.

The memory from last year of how she had wanted to change the Christmas decorations to purple and match the décor in the newly painted lounge came into her mind. She snorted, why on earth would she want to replace all these beautiful mementos with purple tinsel?

The rest of the changes she'd longed for were equally ridiculous. She raged at herself in disgust. Meaningless cards printed on a computer when she had all these beautiful cards with handwritten messages from people that cared about them. And a whole salmon for Christmas lunch? Salmon was for summer, and it could never replace the look of pride on Michael's face when he carried his turkey to the table for their parents.

The memories of all their past Christmas's together nearly choked her. She had been such a fool wishing for change when she should have known that she already had the best Christmas anyone could ever wish for. And, she sighed, more importantly, she'd had Michael.

Chapter Twenty-Four

Michael sat outside the house in his car watching the windscreen wipers go back and forth against the rain. He'd driven slowly back from Ragdale Hall praying and hoping he was doing the right thing. He knew it wouldn't be easy and would have to reach deep down inside himself to forgive what she'd done, but at the same time he couldn't bear the thought of living without her.

He missed her arms wrapped around him through the night as she clung to his back. He missed her breathing and slight snore on his shoulder. He missed her smell and her throaty giggle on a morning. In fact, he sighed, he missed everything about her. She was his best friend.

*

Suddenly, the sound of a car on the drive made her peek between the blinds and her heart began to thump. It was him. Was he returning for more clothes and the rest of his things? She grabbed a tissue from the box and dried her wet face.

'Hiya,' he said, stepping slowly through the doorway into the lounge.

He looked tired. She wanted to wrap her arms around his neck and cling to him for ever. She smiled back and fought the urge to rush at him. 'Hello,' she muttered.

'I needed some time to think,' he said and took another few steps towards her in front of the tree.

She held her breath but nodded in understanding. She put her sweaty hands behind her back and clasped them together as if she was praying. If he were leaving her for good, this might be one of the last times that she would ever see him. She fought back tears and swallowed a huge lump in her throat. Huskily, she croaked, 'Of course you did.'

*

He searched her face relishing in the fact that it hadn't changed in the two days he'd been away. He had missed her so much and took a deep breath. He needed to take his time and gauge her reaction.

'Well, I don't know if I'll be able to forgive what you've done but I want to try,' he said then paused. 'That's if you think we could make it work because I still want us to be a family.'

She gasped in shock and placed a hand over the baby. Her face paled and he dashed to her side. The thought that there was something wrong with either of them scared the hell out of him. 'What is it? Are you okay?'

She giggled. 'Yes, the baby must be moving around, I think. It was just like a fluttering sensation, but they told us at the ante natal to expect that, so it should be okay.'

His heart slowed and he looked at her beautiful face. It was true what everyone said about pregnant women. She did have a shining glow about her that was utterly charming, and he felt his eyes brim with tears. He wanted to be part of this newness and didn't want to miss any of the happenings. 'C…can I feel it?'

She nodded. 'Oh, Michael,' she whispered. 'I'll never forgive myself for hurting you so much but if you could just give me another chance, you'll never regret it, I promise.'

With one hand along her shoulder, he inhaled her smell and felt his shoulders relax just at being close to her again. Gently he placed his other hand over the baby and felt the fluttering movements. 'It's certainly doing a jig in there,' he mused. 'Look, I know we've got a lot to talk through, Davina and I know this baby is probably not even mine. But I will love little junior no matter what happens.'

*

She closed her eyes in pleasure at his touch on her body. His Hugo Boss aftershave filled the space between them, and she sighed at his familiarity and closeness. 'I love you so much, Michael,' she said.

They slumped down onto the settee together and he ran his hands through her hair. 'It's okay,' he said mumbling into her neck. 'We don't even have to do this DNA test, as far as I'm concerned, that's if you don't want to?'

Tears pricked the back of her eyes at his words knowing how difficult it must be for him to accept what she'd done. He was a proud man, and she knew this was costing him dearly. She swallowed hard, dreading having to mention Stewart's name, but knew honesty was the only way forward.

She took a deep breath and stammered, 'S…Stewart has threatened to get in touch in the New Year, and as much as I'd love him to disappear off the face of the earth, I know he's going to want to know the results next July. He also warned me that he'll want to take the baby to Spain to meet his parents which scares the life out of me!'

*

He watched her chew her bottom lip and saw tears brim in her eyes with fear. Thinking of the big oaf menacing his beautiful wife he pulled his shoulders back, 'Oh, did he? Well, from now on, Davina, if Stewart rings, texts or turns up here we face him together, as a family,' he said firmly and tightened his arms securely around her.

He felt her soften and relax in his arms and he stroked her hair.

'If he insists upon DNA and, if the baby does turn out to be his,' he said then paused for breath thinking of a solution. 'Well, he must be allowed access of course, but it will be done properly through a solicitor, and our baby goes nowhere without one, or both of us, being present.'

*

She placed a hand upon his chest and sighed with relief that he was going to stand by her and knew it was more than she could have ever hoped for. He was like her knight in shining armour. She looked up into his face and smoothed a hand down his cheek into his goatee beard. 'Well, if it is his, then the baby will be lucky enough to have two fathers, but you'll always be the main one, Michael,' she said stroking her bump. 'Because you're the man we both truly love.'

If you have enjoyed this story - A review on amazon.co.uk would be greatly appreciated.

You can find another Christmas story from Susan Willis here:

The Christmas Tasters https://amzn.to/3jlTooL

Plus

An award-winning food lover's romance novel, 'NO CHEF, I Won't! https://amzn.to/3jefd0M

A psychological suspense novel, Dark Room Secrets https://amzn.to/3q9jl1M

An award-winning novella with Free recipes inside, Northern Bake Off https://amzn.to/2Ni4xQy

Website www.susanwillis.co.uk

Twitter @SusanWillis69

Facebook m.me/AUTHORSusanWillis

Instagram susansuspenseauthor

pinterest.co.uk/williseliz7/